The Wishing Year

by Winifred E. Wise

cover and decorations
by Olindo Giacomini

WHITMAN PUBLISHING COMPANY • Racine, Wisconsin

Contents

1   *Three Wishes*

When Cheryl Kramer opened the box of breakfast cereal that Friday morning, she found a wishing ring inside, encased in a cellophane envelope. "All this junk you get in the cereals," she said with the scorn of her fifteen years. "Airplanes and Indians and monkeys and I don't know what next for the kiddies. Who'd believe in a wishing ring?"

She tossed the purple plastic article aside and sipped at her orange juice which was the frozen kind she preferred because it didn't have bits of pulp in it like the fresh. People here in southern California could rave all they liked about the virtues of orange juice fresh from the trees in their yards, but Cheryl considered this nonsense.

No one in the Kramer household ordinarily paid much attention to the others at this hour of the day, and she didn't expect an answer. She was only half-awake herself, as was Mother. Only Father had yet begun to bloom. As he put down his newspaper to pour himself another cup of coffee, the scent of his shaving lotion drifted across the table, and Cheryl blew him a kiss. He was the lean, athletic type, and so good looking and comparatively young for a father that all her friends envied her. Sometimes they even flirted with him a little, just for practice . . . a father was safe.

Father wasn't a flirt, but he was an attractive man. Cheryl wondered whether Mother had had any trouble snaring him. Mother was never at her best at the breakfast table, but Father didn't seem to mind. All the newspaper columnists—whom Cheryl and her closest friends Judy Adams and Alicia Marsh read avidly for romantic advice—preached that wives should look their prettiest in the mornings before the couple parted for the day, and the three of them agreed this was the least a woman could do.

"A wishing ring?" Mother came alive suddenly. "Do you suppose it will work?" Playfully, she tried it on for size and then raised her voice. "Look, George, I'm wishing."

"Go right ahead. Nobody's stopping you." He smiled

tolerantly as he put down his paper and assumed what Cheryl thought of as his "let's be kind to Mother" look.

"I wish—oh, I do wish—you'd get that promotion. You've earned it a dozen times over—"

"Thanks for the kind thought, dear, I can use it." He patted her hand and returned to his reading. There was little enough time for it in the mornings before he left for Los Angeles.

"Aren't you going to wish for anything, Cheryl?" Whenever Mother discovered a new game, she always wanted everyone to join. Her lips parted with interest as she turned to her daughter, her vivacity brightening what was otherwise a monotonous effect. Pale lips, pale skin, pale scarf over ash-blond hair still in bobby pins. Mother never used makeup in the early mornings, never cared how sloppy she looked.

It was only in the past year that Cheryl had grown so critical of Mother; she wished she would wear something at the breakfast table other than an old gray shirt and flannel slacks. Cheryl was critical of everyone nowadays, especially of herself. Mother said this was part of growing up, but that didn't make it any the less painful for everyone concerned.

"Don't tell me you have everything you want . . . that you've nothing to wish for." Mother was persistent.

Cheryl poured cream on her cereal with a deliberation that would give her time to choose from her secret desires . . . pick one from her throbbing hoard of them that would not give rise to a teasing that—as she knew all too well—could bring sudden tears. The Kramers could be rough on each other, all in the name of fun, and Cheryl was thin-skinned. She could cry these days over the least little thing. Oversensitive was the word Mother used.

She'd have to say something now, and what could it be? Something that would satisfy Mother's curiosity, not make her feel that you were holding back a thing she ought to know. Mother had an uncanny way of penetrating to your weakest points, reading your innermost thoughts. It must be her womanly intuition of which she had a complete set, as Father often said in vexed admiration. Mother was devoted to them both—Cheryl was sure of that—but she could overdo it by trying to climb right into your skin.

"For heaven's sake, dear, don't make us wait all day. We've other things to do, you know." Mother was growing impatient. "Whatever is it that you have on your mind . . . what dreadful revelation?"

"I—I wish I was a whole lot thinner. Thin and, well . . . interesting looking. You know what I mean." There, she'd said it, and they could laugh all they liked. "Not such a great big ox."

"I like you just the way you are," Father said loyally, with not so much as a grin. "You look strong and healthy, and I can't stand scrawny girls. Like that Ethel Barnes, for one. Or some of your mother's friends. Starving themselves just to. . . ."

When Mother appraised you, as she was doing now, you might as well be standing in front of a mirror and taking a full-length view. Cheryl could see herself just as she was: an overgrown girl who had not yet gotten rid of her "baby fat." A girl who slumped when she should sit tall and who must remember to pull in her stomach.

Cheryl knew, without Mother's telling her, that she could avoid the splotches that marred her olive skin by scrubbing with soap and water, and not eating chocolate. She knew she should have washed her hair last night and set it. Now her short dark locks hung about her face in unbecoming strings, and she'd have to wear a headband.

The girl that Cheryl saw mirrored in her mother's eyes was not doing all that she could to improve her appearance. The worst of it was that Cheryl was well aware of this. Mother didn't need to remind her again.

"You have only yourself to blame, my dear." Mother was stating the obvious. "Look at your cereal. You've soaked it with sugar and drowned it in cream. If that's your idea of a way to thin down. . . ."

"Yes, Mother." Cheryl stared at the offending cereal bowl and hoped that Mother wouldn't have time this morning to launch into the subject of "advantages"— all the things that she and Father were trying to give her, little luxuries which they'd never had at her age.

"Isn't anyone going to kiss me good-bye?" Father stood up and stretched. He was about to take off for his office miles away in the big Los Angeles mail-order house, driving the crowded freeway that led to the city in what Mother termed "the morning suicide race." Cheryl had a too-vivid picture of what could happen on the freeway during the rush hours, morning and night. Overturned cars . . . cars in flames . . . ambulances hurtling to the rescue amidst the blood-curdling screams of their sirens. If only her father had a job here in nice, quiet, stodgy old Belmont Beach where he'd be safe! Mother was always asking him to make the change, but he said he'd earn less money here.

"Drive carefully, Dad." Cheryl brushed his ear with her lips. It had been a long while since she'd had to stand on tiptoe to do it.

"Take care of yourself, dear." Mother always had a worried tone in her voice as she bade him good-bye. "Come back safe."

The familiar words had a warm ring to them as the Kramers began to scatter for the day in their several directions. Father usually traveled farthest, but sometimes Mother went an even greater distance. During the season, she modeled for smart dress houses as far up as Beverly Hills, but today she was staying in Belmont Beach to do a show for one of the local department stores. She need not report there until noon. She could drive Cheryl on to high school . . . stop at the hairdresser's . . . pick up the dry cleaning and. . . . Mother always organized her day so as not to lose a precious minute.

"Better if you walked." Cheryl had known she'd say that. "You'd thin down if you walked every day both ways. That is, if you didn't stop at the Chocolate Shop or the Hamburger Choo-Choo or whatever."

"That's after school. They're not open in the mornings." Cheryl was already cross at herself for having opened again the subject of her weight. Now Mother would make an issue of it and never let it rest. "I walk about a thousand miles a day as it is . . . you should try it sometime. You need track shoes to get to all of your classes—one end of campus to the other. And, besides, if you don't drive me, I'll be late. I've missed the bus, and I've three tardies already this month."

It was another of those beautiful sunny days in California when all the world sparkled and, as an extra dividend, the air was so clear and free from smog that you could see across the miles to snow-covered mountains. On such a day of bright blue sky and dreamlike vistas, it was a shame to spend so much as an hour inside any one of the ugly classroom portables that dotted the campus of Hunterford High.

As Cheryl and her mother drove near, she could see the lines of students streaming antlike toward the high school building itself, a long outmoded and long since outgrown structure of stucco and tile popularly known as the "Spanish Horror." It dated from the days when much of the architecture of southern California had been pseudo-Spanish, and when architects had gone wild over bell towers and arcades, like those on the old missions. The windows were small and narrow; the main doors were constructed of heavy timbers, so dark and so forbidding that they might well have led to dungeons. Students solemnly affirmed that they did. They further maintained that, on stormy winter nights, you could hear the prisoners groan.

The car was drawing to a stop when Cheryl caught her breath so sharply that her mother looked at her anxiously. "Whatever is wrong with you, Cheryl? You're not getting an attack of your asthma, are you? I thought you'd outgrown it."

"Nothing's the matter, and thanks for the lift, Mom. See you tonight."

"Have a good day, dear," Mother called after her. "All your days should be happy at your age."

Little did her mother know. She'd grown up in the days when Belmont Beach was far smaller, and she could have no idea what it was like now to be a sophomore, lost in the shuffle of thousands of students. Hunterford High had grown so fast in the past few years, with all the people pouring into southern California from other parts of the country, that city fathers were aghast at the student horde and hard put to take care of it.

Nor could Mother possibly remember what it was like to be fifteen and have a crush on a boy who didn't know you existed . . . a boy who made your breath come fast and your heart pound whenever you so much as glimpsed him. Bill Meyers, debater and upperclassman. He was walking ahead of her with that long easy stride of his. If she hurried, she might be so fortunate as to reach the wrought-iron gate just ahead of him.

He'd hold it open for her . . . she was sure of that. Bill Meyers would have beautiful manners, manners to match that speaking voice of his which vibrated through the high school auditorium and reached even to the farthest rows of the balcony and to the lowliest of the low . . . the sophomores.

Bill Meyers was always being called upon to address high school assemblies during clean-up weeks and paper drives and such. Even to these mundane subjects, he brought the same ardent spirit that he showed on the debating platform in serious topics like: "Why Red China should, or should not, be admitted to the United Nations." Whatever Bill Meyers talked about, he could thrill you, make you believe that the side he took was the right one.

What more could a girl wish, really, than a date with Bill Meyers? This was close to the top of Cheryl's private list of desires . . . sometime, somewhere. Whenever her grandmother played that old scratched record of hers, "I'm Always Chasing Rainbows," Cheryl, of recent months, had thought only of Bill.

Though she had tried to tell herself that the whole idea of a wishing ring was silly, she was glad now that she had picked it up from the table at the very last minute and brought it along. As she fumbled to get it out of the pocket of her bulky sweater, others crowded between her and Bill, so that she had lost her chance for close contact. No matter . . . the wishing ring was on her finger, and she pressed upon it hard.

As anyone who had ever read fairy tales knew, a person could have but three wishes and must be careful not to waste them. It was much too bad, nowadays, that the whole idea of fairy godmothers had gone quite out of date, she thought, her spirits lifting none the less as she played with this childish nonsense.

At any rate, the ring would be something to talk about when she met Judy and Alicia at lunchtime, something to add to their daily reading of the lovelorn columnist and their horoscopes from the pages of the Los Angeles paper which Alicia always remembered to bring. It just could be that this was a lucky day for those born under the Libra sign. Cheryl and Judy were Libras, and Alicia was Capricorn.

That was one of the first things they had discovered about each other when they met last fall in physical education . . . three girls from three different junior high schools suddenly cast adrift upon the stormy, bewildering seas of Hunterford High. You had to make new friends quickly because lots of your old ones didn't fit any more. Like Ethel Barnes, for example. Ethel had attended summer school and had been tutored so that she could be a junior and ahead of her class for her age. When they met on the street, she never let you forget it. She was a junior, and she was a sorority girl.

"Must be they asked her because her father is a dentist," Cheryl's father had commented when told about the sorority, this latest in Ethel's growing list of achievements. "He has pull."

Father made dreadful puns and shouldn't be encouraged, Mother had said, giggling in spite of herself. Cheryl's family could laugh about the most serious things and make light of them . . . things that could mean life or death to a girl's social success.

Now that she was in the second semester of her sophomore year, Cheryl had come to think that belonging to a sorority must be the magic key to popularity and happiness. It seemed to her that you never could "be anybody" in high school unless you belonged to one of them. The sorority girls were the ones who drove up to school in the most expensive cars and wore the best-looking clothes. They were the ones who were conspicuous in campus activities and dated the fraternity boys. By some mysterious process which Cheryl did not understand but which she longed to undergo, ordinary girls were transformed almost overnight into seemingly glamorous creatures.

Though fraternities and sororities were officially frowned upon by school authorities, they flourished the more because they were supposed to be "secret." Practically everyone knew who belonged to them. And it was recognized that they controlled many of the class elections. Most schools had ruling cliques of some kind, her father said, adding that he had never liked them. When he was in high school, he and his friends had been proud to be "independents." They weren't going to let anybody who fancied himself to be a "high and mighty mucky-muck" tell them whom they should vote for and what girls they should date.

"Hope you aren't getting any of that kind of rubbish into your head," he had said, referring again to Ethel Barnes. "Who is she to order you around?"

Racing from her homeroom today to get to her science class on time, she all but ran into a group of girls from one of the sororities who were sauntering along at a far more ladylike pace. She felt that they were observing her critically, sizing her up and down as a prospect, all but writing down marks in a little black book.

This was the season of the year, just before the spring rushing teas, when sophomores were being screened for invitations. As Cheryl looked now, she'd never receive one. She'd dressed in such haste that her sweater was the wrong color to match the plaid of her skirt . . . her hair was a mop . . . her comfortable old flats were unpolished. Suddenly, she was so conscious of the bad impression she must be making that she could not remember even one name of the several girls whom she knew. She flew past them with merely a "Hi."

It was no way to act, she told herself later in science class, as she adjusted her microscope and looked down at the slide where a flea was entombed. She should have been gay and casual in passing, tossing over her shoulder some such remark as, "Isn't it perfectly mad?"

She was an A student in science, but she would flunk in what mattered far more to her this spring if she didn't watch out. She'd be lost in her homework, first thing she knew, while all the world danced merrily on its way and left her so far behind that she'd never catch up with it. "Who was that dreary girl we used to know? I'd quite forgotten about her. Whatever happened to Cheryl Kramer?"

When the bell rang at the end of science class, she ducked into one of the washrooms to powder her nose and add lipstick. It was the least she could do before she went out again to join the general stampede. Heaven knows, it was bad enough even in the washroom with a dozen other girls crowding about the mirror to make similar hasty repairs.

Cheryl's next classes were all in those loathsome gray portables that made the whole campus look like a concentration camp. You had to travel so fast and so far that you could scarcely make roll call, much less catch your breath. Besides, she was famished; and, as the various clocks crawled toward the noon hour, she regretted leaving half of her breakfast uneaten. Thinning down was the least of her worries now as she thought longingly of lunch.

When finally she was able to join Judy and Alicia in the line that milled outside the entrance to the school cafeteria, she felt on the verge of collapse. "Hold me up, will you? I'm dying."

"Have to save my strength for getting inside." Alicia was always matter-of-fact. Seeing an opening closer to the door, she dodged into it with her friends close behind.

Though the special for today was even more repulsive than usual—lamb stew in a dishrag gray color dotted with poisonous green peas—it was a step above utter starvation. And it was not until Cheryl was mopping up her plate with the last of her rolls and half of Judy's that she again thought of the wishing ring.

"Whatever's that?" Judy cried, seizing upon the odd-looking object as she tossed it upon the table. "Something you got out of a gum machine?"

"Of course not." Cheryl pretended indignation.

"Don't you know a wishing ring when you see one?"

"Might come in handy, at that." Judy fingered the snakelike carving that encircled it, her blue eyes sparkling with interest. "When do we start?"

"Gives you three wishes, but you can't break the cycle." Cheryl warmed to her subject. "It has to be mine until I've made three."

"I could use a few wishes," Judy said, surrendering the ring to Cheryl. "Hurry up, will you? I'm next."

"I've only one more, and I'm not going to tell anybody what it is." Cheryl wrote hastily upon a scrap of paper which she folded and creased. "You'll have to guess."

"What else is there to wish for except one gorgeous male?" Judy heaved a deep sigh.

"Old enough to drive a car." Alicia added the essential element. What good was a boy if parents had to drive you everywhere?

Cheryl shook her head. "I wished that the second time round. But we've talked about this third one almost as much." Her heart was set upon this third wish of hers. She had to belong to a sorority, or she would never survive.

But she'd never admit it now that Feeney Chase had stopped beside their table with her tray, pretending again that she could find no other place to sit. The name of Feeney was bad enough—short for Josephine —but Feeney herself was worse. She was always tagging after them and trying to elbow her way into their close little group. So far as Feeney Chase was concerned,

Cheryl thought, four was a crowd.

Cheryl tore her paper slowly into bits. No, she wouldn't tell anyone now what her third wish had been. Mother always said that she wanted things too hard, and perhaps she was perfectly right.

2 *Encounter with Ethel*

If you belonged to a sorority, you'd likely be doing something exciting every weekend, Cheryl thought, as the last class was dismissed. Strolling across campus to her locker, she felt the weight of her books. Other girls had boys eager to carry theirs. Other girls were making dates, she was sure, as catcalls and giggles filled the corridor with all the gay sounds of late Friday afternoon.

It seemed to her that she was the only student in the school who was going to stay home tonight and watch television. She had nothing ahead of her but television

—and helping with the housework tomorrow and weeding the lawn. And on Sunday she'd have to drive over to see some friends of her mother's if she could think of no way to get out of it. She wasn't a little girl any more . . . she didn't have to go everywhere with her parents, did she? You could overdo this "togetherness" routine when you were fifteen years of age.

The weekend stretched before her like a wasteland, so devoid in prospects for fun and amusement that even staying in school might be preferable. And now, as though to make matters worse, she could see that Ethel Barnes was bearing down upon her.

It was too late now to pretend that she hadn't seen Ethel . . . too late to become absorbed in that faded old mural which stretched along the opposite wall and which showed Spanish cavaliers on horseback, surrounded by Indians and Franciscan fathers and funny old ox-carts in some kind of jumble that was supposed to mean something but doubtless never had to the generations of students who had tramped along below it. Besides, most of the characters in it looked cross-eyed, Cheryl thought, trying in vain to ignore Ethel. In all these months since she had occupied this wretched old locker that stood across from the wall-piece, she had never scrutinized it so closely. The Spanish occupation of California, or whatever it represented, could not have been nearly so difficult as her daily chore of fighting to open and close this scarred metal hulk.

No, she could not escape Ethel; she was trapped. In her present mood, she was not prepared to be civil.

"Haven't seen you in ages," Ethel said, opening the conversation in friendliest fashion. "Where have you been keeping yourself?"

When Ethel was friendly these days, she always had a reason for it, Cheryl had discovered. She was not so naive about Ethel as once she had been. Ethel always had an angle.

"I've been around, same as usual."

Ethel gushed on, obviously not interested in what Cheryl might say. She kept glancing over her shoulder, as though she were waiting for someone, and her words had a hollow ring to them. "We must get together. Seems these days I've no time at all."

She turned away suddenly to link arms with a boy of no particular charm except that he was a "letter" man. His sweater bore the H that marked him as one of the school's leading athletes. " 'Bye now," she called back to Cheryl.

The boy had not been in pursuit of Ethel. He had been loafing along, and he seemed surprised by this encounter, and puzzled. She was a schemer, Cheryl thought, hoping that the boy had sense enough to realize that Ethel had pounced upon him like—well—like a spider upon a fly.

She was just as quick as all that, and she was also little and what some called "cute"; she'd likely get away with it. Ethel Barnes could get away with murder, and yet there was a pertness and sauciness about her that Cheryl grudgingly admired—that and the way Ethel wore her clothes. She had a trim figure, and she always looked well-groomed, stylish, and neat.

You could never say that Ethel was pretty. Her chin was too square and her eyes were too small. They were tiny eyes, bright as buttons, and at times they had a mean and selfish glint. But, as the saying went, Ethel was a girl who "made the most of herself." And, currently, she was running circles around one Cheryl Kramer—great, wide, and ever-spreading circles. There was not the slightest doubt of that in Cheryl's mind.

Cheryl waited until Ethel and her newest beau, if you could call him that, had disappeared. She'd leave school by one of the side doors, she decided, lest she again encounter them. She'd had more than enough of Ethel for one day. If she never saw her again, that would be quite all right. In fact, it would be perfect.

It was too late to turn back when she saw her mistake. The walk was narrow, and other students were crowding behind her so that she had to press forward. Along the curb, a station wagon was being loaded with sleeping bags and skis and toboggans—all the paraphernalia for a weekend in the snow which, in southern California, meant up in the mountains.

The windshield of the car bore a sorority sticker, and Ethel was part of the chattering group preparing to go on this gay expedition. Cheryl was so close that she could not help but hear tantalizing bits of conversation that involved mountain cabins and a dance at some lodge.

They must be headed for Arrowhead or Big Bear, Cheryl decided, picturing for herself the intimacy of cozy fire circles with sparks flying upward to the branches of majestic pines, of couples drifting away to break trails through the snow and wander romantically under the stars.

"Serves them right if a mountain lion scares them." Cheryl must have said it aloud, for several students turned to stare at her. They must think that she was crazy to be talking to herself. She flushed with embarrassment.

"Don't you think so?" She pretended that her remark had been addressed to a rough-looking boy on a motorcycle.

"How's that?" He shifted his gaze briefly from the traffic light. "Call me up some time," he flung back over his shoulder rudely as he prepared to roar away up the street.

"Don't have your number," Cheryl shouted after him. Her eyes blazed with indignation. Apparently he had taken her for one of those cheap and easy girls, one of those "pickups" who stood around on street corners and went with any boy who whistled at them.

She walked away hastily before she could make further blunders and before Feeney Chase could have a chance to pick up her trail. It would be just her luck this afternoon to have Feeney come bouncing after her with the puppylike adoration that annoyed Cheryl and her friends. She could look at you with such wistful eyes that you felt cruel when you refused her. Feeney was always wanting Cheryl to come over to her house and pop corn or make fudge, but Cheryl had never accepted.

Feeney's suggestions were always too dull and too childish.

It wasn't that she actually disliked Feeney so much as that Feeney practically breathed down your neck. Feeney was so anxious to be a part of Cheryl's small group and share in its secrets that the members put up defenses. Cheryl didn't want anybody to press her too hard.

Too restless to go straight toward her home in Canterbury Knolls this afternoon, Cheryl remembered her grandmother. She had not paid her a visit in weeks, and one was long overdue. Besides, she needed to stretch her legs and take a good long walk to this older section of the town where her father's mother lived and where Cheryl also had lived when her family first returned to the beach town.

Grandmother was always saying they never should have left it for Canterbury Knolls which was shiny and bright and new like so many of the subdivisions that were springing up everywhere among the walnut and the orange groves. Grandmother deplored the changes that were taking place in Belmont Beach, as she deplored extravagance.

"Canterbury Knolls . . . Meadowlark Manor . . . Park Estates," she would say disdainfully, running through the list of the various developments. "Hm-m-ph, what are they but a lot of fancy names? And you pay for them right through the nose."

Grandmother had many ideas about what was wrong with the modern generation, and living beyond your means was one of them. Cheryl found her comfortably rocking on the wide front porch of her bungalow in the old-fashioned chair that was part of a wicker set that, as Grandmother said, had been good to begin with and had "stood up" through the years.

No spun aluminum chairs for Grandmother, no colorful plastic lounges, and, for that matter, no ornately planted patio. A front porch with a canvas swing and stands that burgeoned with begonias was all that anyone needed. What was good enough for folks back in Iowa was good enough for them in California or any other place. Grandmother saw no need for changing with the climate.

Trim and spare in her starched cotton housedress, Grandmother was always ready for afternoon callers though there were not many. She seized upon Cheryl with the eagerness of one who lived too much alone. Cheryl understood about that, knowing that Uncle Elmer couldn't be pleasant company for anyone—and least of all for himself. She wondered whether her uncle was in his room off the kitchen today, and hoped that he wasn't.

Uncle Elmer was the black sheep of the family, and not even Father could say that he amounted to much. Not in these days. Maybe he had been a hero during World War II, but that had been a long time ago. He had been one of those who survived the horrors of the "death march" on Bataan. That was why he drank now, her father explained. He drank to forget.

Mother, too, was sorry for Uncle Elmer, feeling that

the war was responsible for wrecking his life. But, whatever his excuse for behaving as he did, Cheryl could not endure him. She had definite ideas about how adults should behave, and wandering about in a daze half the time was, to her, not sad but unspeakable.

"Elmer's up in northern California, looking for work." Grandmother answered Cheryl's unspoken question. "It gives me a chance to clean up his room and have everything nice for him," she added brightly.

"And throw out all the bottles, I suppose." Cheryl's tone was bitter. "Find them where he's hidden them."

"The young have a hard shell on them, and it takes a bit of living to crack it," Grandmother reproved her gently. "You need to suffer a little, my dear."

"But I do. I suffer all the time about everything. You've no idea. . . ."

"Little things. Little bits of things that aren't worth bothering about." Grandmother grew severe. "You're pampered to death, and that's the truth of it. I never in my born days saw a girl who was more spoiled."

This was one of Grandmother's favorite topics and one of which she seldom tired. Cheryl's parents gave her far too much for her own good, and they would rue the day. Cheryl reached for one of Grandmother's big delicious cookies and prepared for a lecture. The cookies were the molasses kind with raisins and nuts and, according to Grandmother, they had been famous all over Iowa. Grandmother never used cooky mixes; she scorned newfangled shortcuts.

Actually, Grandmother's lectures were often closer

to sermons. As the wife of a country minister, she had struggled on a small and irregular income to raise a God-fearing family, and she colored her conversations with vivid forebodings of doom. Grandmother's was a stern and gloomy faith in which one lived with faint hope of escape from the hellfire and brimstone.

Of her family of five, all had departed from the straight and narrow path which she and her husband had set for them. They were too worldly, too bent upon pleasure and luxury. Because most of them lived in other states and came only for visits, it was Cheryl's parents who bore the brunt of her criticism. Cheryl resented this.

"I can't see there's anything sinful about living in a nice modern house and having a room to yourself. Honestly, Grandmother—"

"With your own bathroom and your own telephone and I don't know what all? When I was your age—"

"It's just an extension," Cheryl defended the telephone. "And Dad uses my bathroom when Mother's in theirs."

"And runs himself ragged trying to keep up with the bills." Grandmother prided herself on never owing a cent. "The same with your mother. Out prancing around with all that modeling of hers to make extra money and—"

"She likes to do it. Likes it better than staying home all the time." Cheryl was filled with deep loyalty. "Don't you understand, Grandma? She's awfully clever, and Dad and I are very proud of her."

"You can't buy happiness with money, Cheryl, and don't you forget that. You can't buy happiness in Canterbury Knolls or any other place on this earth."

False ideals and self-indulgence . . . that was the trouble with the modern age, Grandmother said. All this living today because you'll be gone tomorrow. How had people forgotten that the main thing was to do your duty to your home, your God, and your country?

"Does that make a person happy?" Cheryl didn't intend to sound impertinent. She really wanted to know. Where did happiness come from anyway? Where did you find it, and how? Grandmother, with all of her years and all of her wisdom, should be able to tell her if anyone could.

But Grandmother was rocking back and forth with the faraway look in her eyes and a faint smile on her lips. "Every person has to discover happiness for himself, my dear. No one else can do it for you. Now you run along and get home before dark."

She bestirred herself to pack a shoe box with cookies as a treat for Cheryl's father. Ever since he was a little boy, this kind had been his favorite.

"Did he used to steal them out of the cooky jar?" Father's appetite for cookies was proverbial.

"He was no better than he should be." Grandmother's gray eyes softened. George was her youngest child, the one born so much later than the others that there was a wide gap in years. "I'm afraid I did spoil him because he was the last."

"Maybe like Mother and Dad are spoiling me now

because I'm the only one?" Cheryl couldn't resist the mischievous question.

"Go along with you, child." Grandmother gave her an affectionate pat. "You'll make me miss my TV program." Grandmother loved to watch westerns.

Cheryl skipped down the front steps, swinging the box by its string and relieved that her call was over for today. Grandmother's views were too grim for the young girl's taste, too hard for her to understand fully. Yet Grandmother was so sure in her beliefs that she was, at the same time, curiously reassuring. She was a person who knew where she stood.

Grandmother did as she pleased—wore housedresses to church when she chose, hadn't changed her hairdo in maybe fifty years; she was as set in her ways as the crimp in her snowy-white hair. Yet one had the feeling that she would always be there, solid as a rock. Unlike everyone else, Grandmother never changed. She stimulated and challenged you, even if you did not always agree with "the piece of her mind" which she offered you.

When you walked along the street on which she lived, you had somehow a sense of permanence and home that Cheryl could not explain, but which she liked. Despite the general shabbiness of the area, she preferred it in her heart to Canterbury Knolls where the long, low houses "with every modern convenience" conformed to a similar pattern.

Here, in Grandmother's neighborhood, each house was different. There were cottages almost lost in climbing roses and lovely bougainvillea. There were more pretentious structures of two and three stories with dormer windows, cupolas, even tower rooms. What fun it would be to live in a tower room, Cheryl thought, and climb up a long, winding staircase. To have, perhaps, an attic to explore. She had read about attics and their treasures, and she loved to hear about the long-gone days when everyone had an attic where, with the rain pattering upon the roof, one went to look at old family photographs and dress up in old-fashioned clothes. In southern California, rain was rare; and in the modern houses, attics were nonexistent.

You had space here, too, Cheryl thought, space to run and space to live. Houses sprawled lazily over several lots; they weren't built elbow to elbow so that—as her father often said about Canterbury Knolls—you could practically hear neighbors brushing their teeth.

She remembered the days when she and Ethel lived side by side in just such modest bungalows as the ones she was passing. That was before each of their families "had come up in the world" and moved to more flashy surroundings. She and Ethel had once played paper dolls and jacks and jump rope. Ethel had not seemed to mind that it was always Cheryl who could draw the best dolls and best wardrobes, and beat her at jacks, and jump fifty times without missing once. They used to crawl up into the crotch of the great gnarled pepper tree that was their refuge and, nestling companionably, share all their secrets and declare they'd be "best friends" forever and ever.

That had been a long time ago, almost a third of their

lives away, and doubtless Ethel had forgotten all about
the things they used to do. It was the trouble in junior
high school that had started their separation; and, now
that Ethel was getting to be such a "big wheel," she
wouldn't care to be reminded that she had once been
shy and insignificant.

Cheryl wished she still had a good old pepper tree to
climb; but, in Canterbury Knolls, that was like wishing
for the moon. No giant eucalyptus swayed graceful
branches, either, or dropped the untidy curls of bark
from which to fashion canoes for imaginary Indians.
"Progress" had leveled such great and beautiful trees
as the ones she saw here where the bulldozers had not
come, where time was standing still.

If one could only be a child again, how pleasant that
would be. You could dream about what it would be like
to be grown-up, all the wonderful things one could do.
But you wouldn't be facing it . . . being grown-up, that
is. You wouldn't be right on the edge of it. Cheryl could
feel herself moving ever closer to some kind of precipice
from which she could not draw back.

3 *Canterbury Knolls*

Up there, somewhere in the sunset sky, jet planes were leaving wispy trails that captured the yellow and crimson light in patterns soon to vanish. Cheryl quickened her steps, knowing that Mother always worried about her if she were not at home before dusk and would start calling friends to inquire for her. As though anyone would kidnap Cheryl Kramer who was quite old enough—and certainly big enough—to take care of herself. Mother had such a wild imagination, and she could let it run riot.

Finally, after many turnings, she reached the street that led toward her home. She threaded her way impatiently among a traffic jam of wagons and velocipedes—children were always leaving them out on the sidewalks for someone to trip over. From the look of it, people in Canterbury Knolls would never stop having children. Youngsters were dashing across the street after balls or leaping out from the shrubbery with machine guns and that horrible "ack-ack-ack" that practically split open your ears.

"Oh, for goodness' sake, go on home to supper," Cheryl scolded as one of the desperadoes insisted that she lie down on the sidewalk because he had shot her stone dead. From the height of her fifteen years, she felt almost maternal about these grubby little characters. Didn't anyone ever give them a bath?

She hastened onward, wishing now that she had called from her grandmother's to explain why she was delayed. That was the least she could have done; Mother would scold, and Cheryl knew it. Mother would be right to say that she was frightfully thoughtless. And irresponsible, and all the rest of the rigmarole.

She swung past the carriage lamp on the post that bore the name of Kramer in an Old English script that no one could ever decipher, noting as she did so that the geraniums in the planter below it had withered flowers and leaves. That would mean another task, for tomorrow, probably. She'd worry about that when the time came.

"Hi, Mom," she called as she opened the front door

and remembered not to slam it behind her. It was better, she decided, to strike a bright and casual note to begin with, testing the atmosphere. "Have a good day?"

Her words echoed through the pleasant, but deserted, living room. There was a light over one of the easy chairs and a magazine tossed upon the floor beside it, but there was no sign of Mother. Not here or in the colorful kitchen where curls of celery and carrots were soaking in ice-water, and potato peelings littered the yellow sink. Nothing stirred here except Homer, the turtle, who lived in a bowl beside the cafe-curtained window. He was crawling up the rock that was the throne from which he was in the habit of surveying the world. Now he blinked one evil, reptilian eye.

Though it was not her usual habit, Mother might be taking a nap. She was Sagittarius . . . slow to get moving in the mornings but lively as the day drew toward its close. Sagittarians were all night owls, Mother said.

If Mother were napping, Cheryl was in luck. Her late arrival would be overlooked, and she could cover herself with praise by setting the table without being told. Just to make sure, she tiptoed down the hall, grateful for the wall-to-wall carpeting that muffled her tread, and opened the door to the bedroom across from her own.

Mother was not napping, and hadn't been. No impression marked the quilted spread of green taffeta drawn precisely up over the bolster. Mother's slacks and shirt were thrown untidily across the chaise, and the smell of hair lacquer and perfume lingered—she must have dressed in haste.

"I'm acting just like a detective." Cheryl laughed to herself as she tried to figure out what her mother's timing might be. She must have dashed to the store on some errand, or across the street to a neighbor's. If Cheryl could get into her own slacks and shirt before Mother returned, she might appear to have been as punctual as anyone could ask.

She would definitely have to wash her hair tonight, she decided, completing her change and wrapping a scarf about locks that were suddenly loathsome. Her nails were likewise in deplorable shape. She could spend the whole evening on beauty repairs. That was always something a girl could do when nothing better offered . . . this and washing her lingerie and sewing on shoulder straps. Safety pins tore your slips and your bras, but what else could a girl do about them when they broke during the week as you were dashing about to get dressed?

Faced with an uninspiring Friday night, what did boys do to occupy it? Cheryl paused briefly to wonder. They couldn't spend it all shaving . . . not the boys in her classes. They had more pimples than fuzz; it was an age when nature was cruel to them, Father had explained.

Cruel to all of us, I guess. Cheryl was not prepared to waste her sympathy on BOYS. They could always go out unless they were penniless . . . could always call up some girl. Mother said that she had plenty of time ahead of her for dates . . . that she didn't approve of them anyway, except in a crowd, for girls of fifteen. Mrs. Barnes was making a mistake to let Ethel run around so freely and to boast of her daughter's popularity. Despite such differences of opinion, however, Mrs. Barnes and Mother still belonged to the same bridge club and were very close friends.

Ethel was always creeping into Cheryl's thoughts to make her unhappy and discontented. Determinedly, Cheryl turned to the more immediate problem of where Mother was and what she ought to do about dinner. Wandering back through the family room, she turned on the television set for company and set its volume high. She didn't want to watch the program, but she welcomed the cheerful blast of sound that accompanied her into the dining room where she prepared to set three places.

Mother was using the bowl of artificial nasturtiums today as a centerpiece, she noticed, instead of the daisies or roses. That meant orange place mats, amber glasses, and the yellow pottery plates. Mother was fussy about always picking up the centerpiece colors, though Cheryl and her father couldn't care less. What did it matter when you weren't having company? Who cared that you were using the walnut salad bowl and the salt-and-pepper set which stood so fashionably tall that they were awkward to handle?

As she set the third place, she wondered about Father who was seldom so late. He hadn't said anything about not coming home that she could recall, and Mother's preparations for dinner looked as though she expected him. There was all that celery and carrots, and potatoes for three to be boiled. Exploring further, she found lamb chops taken out of the freezer, along with a package of French-cut green beans.

She was trying to decide whether to make an attempt to cook them and have dinner ready, or whether it would be better to wait. She always made such a mess of the kitchen when she tried to cook. Only Gretchen was happy about such an event—when she burned things she had to give them to Gretchen.

In her haste to change when she came in, she had not missed the little old dachshund. These days Gretchen did not always come to welcome her. She must be asleep in her basket, Cheryl thought. Mother kept it under the water heater in the laundry room so that she'd be cozy, but tonight the basket was empty.

Somewhere, out in the patio beyond, she could hear a faint barking. As she opened the door, Gretchen came racing toward her with a speed that belied her short little legs and fat body. When Cheryl picked her up, she was shivering under the blanket-coat she always wore through the winter months. Mother always protected Gretchen from chill, never let her stay outside when there was the slightest risk of her catching cold.

Now the dog whimpered as though to say that everyone had forgotten her and that her rescue was long overdue. Never had there been such a poor, sad, neglected little dog, her eyes seemed to say.

"That makes two of us," Cheryl whispered in her ear, hugging Gretchen. She was growing extremely worried about her missing mother. It was so unlike her ever to leave Gretchen out in the cold that something strange must have happened.

After giving the little dog warm milk and a rubdown, she went around to draw the curtains across the picture windows against the blackness of the night. Someone could be staring at her from out there in the garden . . . someone might enter if she did not make sure that all of the doors were locked. It was no night to read a mystery story or watch a horror movie . . . that much was clear.

What did a girl do when her mother disappeared? She'd feel foolish calling all around among the neighbors asking, "I've lost my mother. Do you know where she is?"

Canterbury Knolls was so gossipy that it would be only too eager to make a big story out of what could turn out to be a very small matter. Too many people here liked to talk, talk, talk—and spread rumors. If she were not careful, they'd be saying that Mrs. Kramer neglected her daughter, and wasn't it a shame when they'd seemed such a very nice family. Can't afford to take your eyes off teen-agers for a minute, they'd say, or they'd have a wild party.

Cheryl's mood changed to anger. Mother could have left her a note, couldn't she? Mother might have known that she'd worry. There had been no message under the sugar bowl on the breakfast bar . . . or on the kitchen bulletin board . . . or pinned to the fireplace screen. Though Cheryl had earlier exhausted these possibilities, she again made the rounds.

Finally, with no appetite left for dinner, she made herself a peanut butter sandwich and drank a large glass of milk. She needed something to help the hollow feeling that she had, something to keep her mind from dwelling upon the worst that could befall. Father might have been in a frightful accident, and, as for Mother. . . .

Try as she would, as the hours passed, she could not stop recalling newspaper accounts that she'd read. About housewives bludgeoned by sinister strangers, about burglars turned killers, about escaping convicts. . . . Among the lurid details given, there was always "evidence of struggle," but Cheryl had seen none in this neatly ordered house.

Next to Cheryl and Father, her home was Mother's pride. She was always going through the pages of magazines to discover the latest ideas in decoration, the smartest color schemes. The large Renoir print which hung over the sofa had been her most recent acquisition. The frame in what she called "pickled walnut" had been chosen to blend with the "honey beige" of the walls and the carpeting, and she had accented the slip-covered furniture with pillows that picked up the glowing reds and the blues of the scene in a French café.

The living room was getting altogether too many "company manners" to suit Father. But, so long as he had the family room, he did not protest. The family room was a place where a man could kick off his shoes and relax, he said, sprawling there in the evenings upon the rattan furniture among his magazines and record albums. Cheryl longed for him to come in now and spill his pipe ashes all over the vinyl-tile floor. She wouldn't mind a bit cleaning up after him.

Cuddling in his favorite chair before the television set, she stroked Gretchen for comfort and listened for a sound of his car, or of Mother's. Gay voices down the street told her that someone was having a party, and howls to the rear where the Perkinses lived informed her equally that one of the six children was "getting the belt." Too bad the luckless youngster had not been able to escape, Cheryl thought. She was always hoping that Mr. Perkins would trip over something in that cluttered backyard of his and fall flat on his face. When he wasn't beating one of the children, he was swearing at them or quarreling with his wife. The Perkinses were a neighborhood scandal, and everyone wished that they'd move.

The Wallaces, a quiet retired couple who lived next door to the Kramers, had passed around a petition to accomplish this purpose. It had stated in high-flown terms that, since the Perkinses were "ruining property values," they could be termed a "public nuisance" and thus be forced to leave the subdivision. Mr. Wallace had circulated the paper about for signatures, but Father, along with many others, had refused to sign. Live and let live was Father's general idea. His only action had been to build a high bamboo fence to screen their view from the Perkins's junk—old Christmas trees, wagons with wheels off them, all manner of rusty remains.

As Cheryl's thoughts skipped about her current surroundings, they centered upon the Wallaces who were such cranks about tidiness that stepping on their lawn was considered a crime. To avoid trouble, Father always warned guests away from it. Aside from her trips to the beauty parlor several times a week, Mrs. Wallace spent her waking hours raking leaves or washing windows or scolding her husband for tracking mud on the driveway whenever he watered the lawn.

When you had lived next to people for almost five years, you knew their habits. Now Cheryl rebuked herself for not thinking of Mrs. Wallace in the early part of the evening. She was devoted to Mother and thus unlikely to spread evil tales. Cheryl could have inquired of her, but now it was too late.

She wouldn't dream of disturbing the Wallaces when the hour was after nine. The only illumination in the house was that faint night-light they kept in their bathroom. If the Wallaces had not already retired, they would be dressed in pajamas and watching TV. Mrs. Wallace wasn't the sort of person who liked to be caught in night robe and curlers, or called to the phone at this hour.

For all of her fifteen years, Cheryl had never before been left alone to spend a whole night. Sometimes, when Mother or Father were going out to a party, she'd invited another girl to stay with her . . . and she'd done baby-sitting for families of which Mother approved. Mother still supervised her activities so closely that Cheryl was growing to resent it.

Wouldn't Mother ever realize that she was almost grown-up and didn't need to be watched every minute? A night on her own was what she'd been dying to enjoy;

but, now that she apparently had it, she was feeling very differently. She felt like—well, like a turtle that had suddenly lost the shell that protected it. She walked into the kitchen. Homer had retired beneath the lettuce leaf she had given him and, removing it, she thought she saw a quizzical look upon his face.

Gretchen followed along behind her, whining uneasily. The little dog sensed that something was wrong and demanded to be comforted. Perhaps she missed the familiar household sounds and didn't care for these echoes. The drip-drip of the faucet in Cheryl's bathroom which the girl tried to shut off and couldn't . . . the whir of the refrigerator . . . the rustle of a branch against the roof.

Cheryl had turned off the television set, but she flicked it on once more as defense against the odd little whisperings that seemed to come from everywhere. This was a night when Cheryl had the freedom to watch the crime programs to which her mother objected . . . a night when she could stay up for the late, late show and on into the Night Owl Program. She could do as she pleased. But there was no delight in it tonight. Not when she had all this worry at the back of her brain . . . and when she felt so deserted and lost.

A girl never knew how much she counted upon her parents until she didn't have them around her. She never realized how much she loved them and how much she had taken for granted. Cheryl ran through the long list of her faults which loomed black against the virtues of her parents. She was often rude, and she was lazy; she was also ungrateful and selfish. She'd done nothing to deserve such a generous and understanding father and mother.

If she were to lose both of them, Grandmother would say it was a judgment upon her. In this unhappy event, Grandmother would take Cheryl to live with her and Uncle Elmer, perish the thought. Grandmother would "do her duty" by a girl who was being "punished for her sins."

She'd run away first, Cheryl decided . . . run away where no one could find her. To Alaska perhaps, or Hawaii. She'd dye her hair and change her name and begin a new life where—where no one would care whether she lived or she died.

The hot tears welled into Cheryl's eyes and streamed down her cheeks. She'd have no one to listen to her troubles, no loving arms to comfort her.

As her mind played through scene after scene of what the future might hold without her parents, she was writing the script of a melodrama filled with sorrow and heartbreak. In the end, the orphan girl who had taken the name of Gloria Gates would rise above every hardship and privation and become famous. As an actress, maybe, or a scientist. Her daydream fuzzed as to exactly how Gloria Gates would triumph before she came back to reveal herself to Bill Meyers and win his love.

Sitting there in the chair before the television set, she drifted off into the uneasy but many-colored fantasy of dreams. How long she had slept there she would never know. It could have been minutes or hours later when

Cheryl awakened with a start.

She could hear footsteps crossing the living room with a furtive, stealthy tread. Terror froze her as they came ever closer; she could make no move to escape.

"Up pretty late, aren't you, chick?" Father said, as he switched on the overhead light.

4   *"Thar She Blows!"*

"The poor kid was crying her eyes out when I found her." Next day, Father was trying to place all the blame upon Mother. "I had to give her a couple of aspirins to quiet her down. A fine thing. . . ."

But Mother would have none of his censure. Weary as she was, she defended herself. Father had no business going "out with the boys" after the basketball game which he'd refereed. When she'd called him, he had told her he was coming straight home, and she had counted upon it.

Was it her fault that someone in Mrs. Angeleno's family hadn't come to get Cheryl and take her across town for spaghetti dinner? Her fault that Mrs. Angeleno's niece had created such a state of excitement that everyone had quite lost their heads?

It had been, it seemed, a dire emergency. Just as Mother was beginning to prepare dinner, Mrs. Angeleno's niece had staggered across the street crying for someone to take her to the hospital quick. Her husband was out of town, and she had gone into labor a month ahead of her time. The pains were so severe that the baby seemed likely to arrive at any moment. Mother had dropped everything to be of assistance.

She'd called Father and Mrs. Angeleno, and off they had gone. Mrs. Angeleno said she'd come over to lock up the house of her niece . . . leave Cheryl a note . . . take care of the whole situation before she joined them at the hospital. Naturally, Mother had assumed that Mrs. Angeleno had done what she'd promised; and, just as naturally, Mother had waited to try to calm the excitable family when complications developed.

"Fancying yourself an angel of mercy, I suppose." Father could be bitterly sarcastic.

"And what are you? A basketball hero?"

"Earning extra money that way," Father reminded her. "You're always glad enough to have extra money to spend."

They were quarreling like two overtense, overtired people who didn't know how or where to stop, and Cheryl hated to see it. Quarrels were rare in this house, and then they were seldom serious, but, all the same, they put one on edge.

"What was it? A boy or a girl?" Cheryl asked as a slight change of subject.

"One of each," Mother explained further. "The doctor hadn't anticipated twins, and he barely pulled them all through the ordeal."

"Double trouble." Father leaped up from the breakfast table with his meal half-finished and, for further emphasis, slammed the back door.

"He'll get over it, Mom." Cheryl went over to put her arm around Mother. "I'm sorry I got so upset last night." She wanted to add that it was because of her love for them, but this would sound drippy. Best only to give Mother a hug and be glad she was there. That was what was important.

She could see that Mother was exhausted by her hospital vigil which had gone on for most of the night, and what she should do now was to tuck her mother in bed. It was odd how grown-up she felt today—how responsible and strong.

"I know what to do, and I'll do it, Mom. Honestly, I will. I—I sort of want to." She couldn't explain further; there were some things a girl couldn't say because she couldn't quite understand them herself. She actually wanted to vacuum the living room and the hall and do the rest of the Saturday cleaning.

"You're so different today, dear. Whatever has come over you?" Mother had a puzzled look in her eyes as she started to tell Cheryl what to prepare for their lunch.

"I'll make Father take me out for a hamburger. No use to spoil him, is there?"

As she hummed about the living room, her voice keeping in tune with the vacuum cleaner, she was overjoyed at not having to enact the role of Gloria Gates. She'd do all the hard corners today, move out the furniture so that the job would be as thorough as Mother's. Yes . . . she might even go so far as to wax the floor of the family room where she'd huddled last night. It looked so bright today with the sun streaming in through the windows that she could almost laugh at her earlier sinister thoughts. But not quite. They had been too vivid to vanish entirely.

Still with a memory of her fears, she sought out Father to make sure of him. She could hear him hammering furiously; Father always hammered when he was angry. He was in his workshop out there in the garage, and he was making a birdhouse.

"Going to get martins this year, Pop?" Cheryl shouted to be heard above the noise.

"We'd jolly well better." Father stopped his work, but he did not look up. "We'd better get real birds before your mother insists on china ones."

"Uh-huh." Cheryl agreed with him. It was altogether too silly the way some people in this neighborhood cluttered up their rooftops with pottery pigeons and storks.

"She all right?" he muttered through a mouthful of nails.

"Why, sure, why shouldn't she be?"

"Just wondered, that's all. Doesn't a man have a right

to wonder a little about his wife?"

With his rumpled hair and in his Saturday sweat shirt, Father looked almost boyish, and Cheryl felt a surge of pride in him. He didn't have a paunch like the fathers of most of her friends, and he wasn't losing his hair. With his trim athletic figure, you could almost mistake him for a college man.

"D'you think the birds should have windowboxes?" Father stopped his work to show her a blueprint that suggested them. Windowboxes and shutters and even a TV aerial. All of which, as Cheryl and her father agreed, was ridiculous. Still, Mother might find it amusing.

"Why not give it the works?" They said it together.

Heavy cleaning was more exhausting than Cheryl had realized, and she had not started on her own room before she collapsed. No wonder Mother was always complaining about the drudgery involved in keeping house and saying that men made such a mess of things. Cheryl was ready to scream at her father for tracking in on her clean kitchen floor.

"If you want any lunch, you'll have to make it yourself." She stuck her head through the door. Father could cook, but he hated it except at a barbecue.

As she had hoped, he preferred to take her out to a hamburger stand. When she was with Father, she could order deluxe with cheese and double the French fries; she could even end up with a malt. Cheryl considered this last possibility as she sat in the sunshine at one of the weather-scarred tables.

"Your mother and I were going fishing this afternoon,

but I guess that's out of the question." Father scowled. Mother had upset all his plans.

"Pier or boat?" Cheryl wanted to know.

"Boat. We thought we might see a few whales thrown into the bargain."

Whales? They were migrating southward at this time of year, Father explained, and many had been seen off the coast. Big gray whales . . . pilot whales . . . traveling thousands of miles from the Aleutian Islands to the gulf of Lower California. "They go down there to have their young every year." Father grimaced. After last night, babies of any kind were still a sore point.

"How about my going with you?" Cheryl's interest was aroused. Fishing bored her mostly, but whales were quite a different affair.

"Got yourself a date." Father slapped his knee as he called for the check.

As luck would have it, they found Dr. Barnes sitting on one of the benches at the end of the pier waiting for the deep-sea fishing boat to return from an earlier expedition. He'd be sure to tell Ethel that he'd seen her, and Ethel would have another chance to feel superior. She was off on a mountain house party whereas Cheryl still had to depend upon her father for amusement. The thought of Ethel appeared like a cloud over the sunny afternoon. Could Cheryl never escape her?

Dr. Barnes greeted them cordially. "Thought I was going to be alone," he said. "My womenfolk don't care much for fishing or boats."

Cheryl left them chatting while she cruised about to

inspect the rest of the passenger list. They were mostly middle-aged couples dressed in the nondescript fashion of folk who placed comfort ahead of fashion—the women with hats firmly tied on their heads and wearing ill-assorted sweaters of every kind and description, the men in shabby jackets. A few girls about Cheryl's age had stopped to read the sign that said COME OUT TO SEE THE WHALES, but, after glancing over the crowd, decided against buying tickets. "Whale-watching is for the birds," one of them said as they walked away. "I want to watch boys."

Cheryl couldn't say that she blamed them. All the handsome male specimens seemed to be out in the harbor riding on water skis or doubtless aboard the sailboats scudding along before the stiff breeze. None at all were pushing against the ropes that led down to the *Sea Queen* landing. As the vessel came about with a skillful maneuver and approached the pier, Cheryl could see that she should have gone on the earlier trip. Several good-looking boys had been aboard and now were preparing to leave, carrying gunnysacks loaded with fish.

Now Dr. Barnes was taking her arm because, as he remarked somewhat wistfully, "Your father and I are sharing girls this afternoon. You don't mind, do you?"

"Of course not." Cheryl would have preferred to be the chosen companion of someone other than a middle-aged father, but she did not wish to be rude. She'd always been fond of Dr. Barnes; he was the family's dentist and had filled her teeth ever since she'd been old enough to have cavities. One of the pictures displayed in his office was a photograph taken of her and of Ethel when they were about eight years old. It was the summer when neither of them could eat sweet corn, and it was entitled "The Toothless Age."

Gallantly escorted by Dr. Barnes, she walked up the teetery gangplank to join her father at the stern. Each of the men carried a pail that was loaded with bait. As Cheryl examined them, she was glad she had told Father to include her out when he rented the poles and the deep-sea tackle. No, thank you . . . thank you very much. She was not about to bait a hook with slimy bits of eel and squid and bloodworms.

Escorted by a screaming flock of sea gulls, the *Sea Queen* moved out across the harbor past freighters with foreign flags and insignia and past pleasure boats, heading for the lighthouse that marked the opening in the great breakwater that led to the open sea. Except for one trip to Catalina Island whose dim outlines showed in the distance, Cheryl had never been out on the mighty Pacific. Now, as the powerful swells came toward them, she realized that she might regret her decision to come.

Mother and Father were fond of deep-sea fishing, but they'd always left her at home and with reason. She'd gotten dreadfully seasick on that trip to Catalina and disgraced the whole family. Now Father, apprehensive that she might repeat the performance, suggested that she should go forward and watch from the bow. Keeping your eyes on the horizon helped to calm your stomach; the horizon was the only thing that did not move in all this seething, watery world.

The ship was swaying from side to side in the heavy swells, and it was with a good deal of difficulty that Cheryl began to follow her father's directions. She was inching along with a firm hand on the rail when a voice called, "Can I help you?"

She could see no one paying special attention to her, and she was about to ignore the voice when she caught sight of eyes staring at her from the porthole of a structure that led down to the inner recesses of the vessel. She saw the coils of rope and the moving pistons of the engine, but she noticed no human figure until a boy in a greasy crew cap scrambled up the ladder and bowed low before her. "At your service, ma'am."

He was a slim youth about half her height, Cheryl figured at first. But, as he straightened up, she thought he could have been half a head taller. Size was hard to determine because a shock of black hair stood up all over his head like a porcupine's bristles and because, as she noted, he was wearing high-heeled boots.

"Ah'm just a sea-goin' cowboy, ma'am," he drawled in exaggerated western style.

Clearly, she had dredged an odd character from the depths of the *Sea Queen,* and she wasn't at all sure that she liked this newest turn of events. "I can manage all right by myself," she said stiffly.

"Sho' nuf, ma'am." He grabbed her arm as she lurched sideways with the pitching of the ship. "Ladies have their cherce."

He sounded like a bad western movie, and she was not amused. He'd hang onto her all afternoon, she thought, and she wouldn't be able to escape. She didn't care for boys who forced their attentions upon you.

"I came with my father," she said to discourage him. When a girl was well chaperoned. . . .

"Fathuh, deah," he said, switching to a phony British accent. "Deah, deah fathuh."

"Are you an actor or something?" In spite of herself, Cheryl could not help a flicker of interest. He didn't sound exactly like a common dockhand or wharf rat. Sorry, but she was a bit of a snob.

"Or something . . . name of Peter Guinness. The New York Guinnesses, of course, no relation to Alec." He spoke in the more normal tones of a boy obviously bored with disclaiming any connection with the famous British actor.

He could be about her age, or he could be considerably older; Peter had a pixie quality about him that defied any definite classification. And now, as he darted away to meet orders from the skipper, she regretted that she'd not been more cordial. It was one of her failings. She was always acting cold and distant with boys to cover up the fact that she was shy inside and didn't know quite how to act. Now she had lost what could turn out to be an interesting prospect.

He paid her little further attention as the boat came to anchor at the edge of the kelp beds which had been their destination. This was where the best fishing was to be found, her father had explained. The smaller fish hid in these forests of kelp to escape from the larger fish which preyed upon them; it was a case of survival.

Fishermen had long observed this.

Acres of rubbery stems and leaves which rose to the surface from some undersea reef calmed the Pacific here, and for this Cheryl was grateful. She could move about the vessel readily and look down into the depths of a shadowy forest airborne by the tiny bubbles which she had so often popped on the beach. The fronds swaying to and fro were dotted with these bubbles dancing everywhere and glistening in the light.

As Father had predicted, the fishing was excellent here, and everyone was busy. Mackerel slithered to the deck . . . slim and silvery forms with the rainbow reflections that made them the most beautiful of any of the fish being caught. Folk were scorning them as "cat food" and tossing them back, but Father was keeping his as a breakfast feast. Nothing could compare with broiled mackerel for breakfast, he said.

Cheryl vastly preferred them to the ugly sculpins that were considered a far greater prize. They were warty and grotesque, as odd as guitarfish, but not dangerous like the sting rays. The sea was like a grab bag, Cheryl decided; you never knew what might come out of it or be tugging at the end of your line. Kelp bass and sand sharks and vicious-mouthed barracuda.

Every now and then she glimpsed Peter cracking ice and throwing it into the bin where the fish were piling up . . . cooking hamburgers . . . pouring coffee. He seemed to be boy-of-all-work around here with no time for anyone but the hungry, middle-aged fishermen. Most of whom were too fat anyway, Cheryl thought, looking them over. She herself had no appetite for a snack. Though she felt better now that the sea was calm, she didn't care for the smell of food.

She wandered from bow to stern and back again, checking on her father and Dr. Barnes from time to time and occasionally looking out across the sea for sight of the whales which everyone else had forgotten. They were all so busy with their fishing in the kelp beds that no one else except Cheryl was even asking about them.

Should a whale come to the surface near the *Sea Queen,* it would doubtless look like an island, Cheryl thought, scanning the glittering blue of the sea for unusual forms other than a freighter which was disappearing below the curve of horizon and faint white puffs that looked like sprays from some fountain. She'd seen several of these in different parts of the sea when Peter appeared at her side.

"Thar she blows!" he cried, rousing the rest of the passengers with a stentorian shout. "Thar she blows-s-s-s-s!"

He sounded exactly like Captain Ahab in the movie *Moby Dick,* Cheryl thought, thrilling to her very toes. She had been first to sight the whale, but now Peter had taken over. The passengers were soon insisting that they go in pursuit of it. Fishing was forgotten as the *Sea Queen* came round and made full speed ahead. From the height of the spouts as Peter described them, the whale, or more likely whales, must be unusually large, the skipper said.

Peter was taking full credit for her discovery, but Cheryl did not mind. What mattered now was to see the whale in person instead of his spout, and to enjoy the porpoises. They had run into a whole school of them, and they were leaping across the waves with effortless ease, like performers putting on a show for an excited audience. Suddenly the ocean was alive with these gay and skillful creatures who performed their antics by twos and by threes with the precision and timing of a ballet ensemble.

Father had been standing behind her, and Cheryl thought that it was his hand she was gripping in her transport of delight. "Look there, and there, and there!"

"Let go, will you?" That was Peter's voice in her ear, and Peter who was pretending to nurse his hand as though she had injured it.

He had no business putting his hand next to hers, and no business now to go through this byplay and make others laugh. Cheryl reddened with embarrassment and walked rapidly away from him. Fancy any girl wanting to hold hands with him, anyway. She could not possibly have hurt him; boys like him were tougher than nails.

He had the audacity to follow her. As she was about to turn to find her father or Dr. Barnes, a great dark form shot skyward, not half a mile distant. Before either she or Peter could utter a word, it hurtled sideways and disappeared.

"Whew-w-w!" Peter was as overcome by the unusual sight as was Cheryl. "Gosh-a-mighty!"

"Was-was that a wh-whale?" Cheryl found her voice.

"No, it was a sardine, stupid. They have extra-large sardines out here. Grow them that way for sandwiches."

Cheryl resented his sarcasm, but she was so eager to learn more about whales that she overlooked it. You rarely saw whales leap clear out of the ocean, Peter explained to her in a different tone of voice. Perhaps it was trying to escape from a killer whale or had been frightened by the sound of the *Sea Queen's* engine. Whales had very keen hearing, and most kinds were as harmless as cows. They traveled in groups, or pods, as protection from the rapacious killer whales who often followed the southern migration and picked up the stragglers.

Doubtless what they had seen had been a gray whale which had become separated from its companions. Now it had gone down to the ocean depths to sound and wouldn't come up again for a good many miles.

Peter was extremely knowledgeable about whales; but he spoiled this pleasant interlude, too, by adding, "Read all about it. If you can read, that is."

He went to answer the skipper's call from the wheelhouse and left her spluttering.

She had been so absorbed in watching for whales, as had the other passengers, that she hadn't noticed the change which had come over the sea. It was gray now, instead of blue, and presently the skipper called a conference. He hated to risk going any farther, he said, pointing to the west where pearly clouds were obscuring the sun and a fogbank was forming. They might be able to make it back to safe harbor before the fog reached them, and again they might not. All they could do now was make a run for it and hope for the best.

Cheryl huddled close to her father as the clammy mist caught them, still well out at sea. It was scary enough to drive in a car through the fog; how could the skipper possibly find where he was going upon this trackless ocean? The *Sea Queen* was keeping up a ceaseless blast with its whistle, and other vessels were answering from somewhere out there. Unseen forms were moving all about them, and each seemed to say, "I'm close—watch out—don't come too close to me."

Finally she made out a blur of lights and, with the *Sea Queen* moving into its mooring, she wanted to be among the first to descend. The latter part of the voyage had frightened her thoroughly, and she was anxious to set foot back on land.

She'd ignore Peter as she left, she decided . . . refuse to take the arm he was gallantly offering to the ladies who fluttered about him there near the gangplank. She was so busy observing that she did not watch her footing . . . did not see the gunnysack full of fish on the deck.

Peter had to catch her before she fell . . . had to take this last chance to goad her. "Whoa there, girl," he said to her as though she were a horse. "Steady now."

If she were a horse, she'd stamp on his foot, give him something by which to remember her. The thought flashed through Cheryl's mind, but she discarded it. That would be making Peter too important, making him think he'd made an impression upon her.

"See you again, somewhere," he called after her

through the enveloping fog of the night.

Somewhere was right . . . it was not likely that they'd ever meet again anywhere. And sometime would be altogether too soon, she told herself.

5 *Burning Questions*

Cheryl's interest in whales had nothing whatever to do with a boy named Peter Guinness who could now be on his way to Lower California with them for all she cared. She would do her next paper for science class on whales, become something of an authority, and try for an A-plus. After all, she had seen a whale, hadn't she?

Alicia was doing hers on earthworms because they had them in their garden and she could observe them. Judy was choosing mosquitoes because she was fascinated by those that bore malaria and yellow fever and by the heroic fight against them in connection with the building of the Panama Canal. Alicia was always the practical one, whereas Judy had a far-flung imagination and an appetite for romance that exceeded even Cheryl's. She wanted to be a writer later on, whereas Alicia was planning on a teaching career.

As the talk among the three friends gathered about the high school lunch table shifted from science subjects to careers, Cheryl wondered for the thousandth time why she couldn't decide what she wanted to be. The future was still as murky as the fog that had rolled in across the ocean on Saturday afternoon; and, as she regaled her friends with an account of that particular adventure, she left Peter out of it.

They'd expect more to have happened than actually did; they would think that she'd goofed because she had found out nothing about him. Where did he live? Did he go to school anywhere? How old was he? Things like that. Alicia would practically have filled out the blanks on a questionnaire, and even Judy would have collected information of some specific nature.

Other girls kept their wits about them, and Cheryl scolded herself for not doing better. She was always going to improve when the situation arose, but never seemed to get to it. She was a hopeless case, no doubt, but there was no point in admitting it unless she were forced to do so. She had, at any rate, grown smart about that.

Living a considerable distance from Judy and Alicia, she rarely saw them over the weekends, so that Mondays were always a time for comparing notes. They could have ridden bicycles to visit each other; but, now that they were in high school, riding bicycles was kid stuff. They did it only around dusk or in their own neighborhoods where no one of importance was apt to see them. Their mothers all said that this was foolish of them— that girls in the best colleges rode bicycles everywhere— but mothers didn't know how easy it was to lose status at Hunterford High.

Not that they had much status to lose, Cheryl thought, again reviewing the problem of sororities. It was always in the back of her mind, and it came to the fore again when Alicia told about her trip to the coffeehouse known as Dante's Inferno. It had been filled with boys and girls from the various fraternities and sororities, and Alicia had felt like an oddball.

She'd gone with a boy she called Willy-Nilly, and it had been family-arranged. Well-meaning parents had thought that the excursion would be good for them both. "You know how *that* is," Alicia said scornfully, tabling any thought of romance.

Judy and Cheryl nodded sympathetically. Families who were friends always thought their sons and daughters should like each other, but neither Judy's nor Cheryl's had yet gone so far as to fix up a date. It seemed that Willy-Nilly had never been out with a girl, and his family had picked Alicia for practice.

"He sure needs a lot of it," Alicia said, giving a play-by-play account of their evening together. Willy-Nilly was the nickname he had been given when he was small.

Although he was now called Bill, he'd always be Willy-Nilly to Alicia.

"Suits him perfectly," Alicia said firmly. She'd had to do most of the talking and pretend to have fun. A girl had to put on an act before all those others from Hunterford High who were laughing and chatting among themselves and wondering, probably, what business Alicia had even coming into the place.

She hadn't wanted to order the *café espresso* which was a feature of Dante's Inferno, and the Italian soft drinks with strange names had been so expensive that she'd only had two. It had been hard to sit doing nothing and staring at all the wall decorations—Frankenstein's monster and others as conceived by an artist, including the whale swallowing Jonah.

"You'd have liked that, I expect," she said to Cheryl. They had even added real ribs from a whale and gilded them. "But I don't think you'd go for the poetry they read. I couldn't understand it."

"I would." Judy had been listening with increased interest. "Reading poetry out loud the way they do in coffeehouses helps you to get the feel of it."

What Alicia had heard on Saturday night had been all about garbage and howling cats and sleeping in the subway, and there had been a lot of sex in it, too. She'd been shocked over some of the passages. If that was modern poetry, she told them, she'd go back to Tennyson.

Bill hadn't cared for it either; he'd been way out of his depth and had looked around for a jukebox. But Dante's Inferno didn't have one—it went in for folk singing. That had been really fun, Alicia admitted. There had been a man with a guitar, and everyone had sung. She had a good voice and had soloed in "Green Grow the Lilacs." "One of the verses, that is." Alicia was always painfully honest. "The rest joined in on the chorus."

On the whole, however, she and Bill had felt so uncomfortable at Dante's Inferno that they wished they had gone to a movie, as Judy had done. "With a cousin ... girl," she added before either of the others could ask.

Coffeehouses were for juniors and seniors and college students, they decided, not envious of Alicia's experience. But it had been interesting to hear, at first hand, about what went on in them. You wanted to know what the outside world was doing, even if you didn't care for this particular part of it.

She would vastly prefer to have gone up to Arrowhead, Cheryl thought, listening to other scraps of conversation circulating about in the school cafeteria. Apparently, it was the Tri Phis and the Gamma Delts who had rented houses side by side for the mountain weekend. Ethel Barnes was a Tri Phi.

"Thanks for letting me use your sleeping bag," Ethel called to Cheryl across the gap that separated them by far more than space between tables. It was the gulf between the insiders and the outsiders, the difference between those who could be smug and self-assured and those who were wistful and envious.

Mother must have lent her bag to Ethel or to Mrs. Barnes and not got around to telling her about it, Cheryl thought, cross at her mother for not asking her first. It must have happened on that Friday afternoon when Mother rushed off to the hospital. Mother probably thought she wouldn't mind, but Cheryl did mind, and terribly. Ethel wouldn't have aired out the bag the way it ought to be aired—and she might have broken the zipper. Didn't Mother know that Ethel could ruin a sleeping bag? Likely she hadn't taken her own because it was already a mess.

Funny Ethel hadn't wanted to borrow her toothbrush, too. That would be exactly like her. As the bell rang for afternoon classes, Cheryl started on her way across campus, too indignant to realize that she was headed in the wrong direction. It would be Ethel's fault if she were late for American literature . . . Ethel's fault, too, that she couldn't remember the part of Edgar Allan Poe's *The Raven* which she had memorized as part of her homework. The verses had gone quite out of her head, and all she could think of now was, "Quoth the raven, never more."

As she sat in the classroom, the poem began to come back to her in the form of a paraphrase:

> Once upon a midnight dreary
> > While I pondered weak and weary (of Ethel Barnes)
> While I nodded, nearly napping
> > Suddenly there came a tapping
> As of Ethel gently rapping—rapping at my chamber door.
> > "'Tis that Ethel Barnes," I muttered.
> "She shall borrow nothing more!"

Scribbling the words down to show them to Judy later on, she giggled out loud. "And what's so funny, Miss

Kramer?" The English teacher always used the formal mode of address, and now she glared at Cheryl through the harlequin glasses that were the one touch of frivolity in her otherwise severe costume.

Miss Haldoran always wore dark suits and man-tailored blouses that, while they might be made of the best materials, lacked feminine charm. She looked like the sort of person who had never been kissed, who wouldn't know what to do with a man if she had one. She might have a "well-furnished mind," but who would like to sit with it all alone? The girls made private jokes about Miss Haldoran, but they respected her knowledge as they bent to her discipline.

"I—I was just reading ahead a little, and I—I got to Mark Twain." Mark Twain was safe because Miss Haldoran idolized him, Cheryl knew, and her book had opened by happy accident to *The Jumping Frog*.

"Exploring on your own, I see. A very good sign." Miss Haldoran beamed. "Let the rest of the class take note."

Apparently, Cheryl had reached the ultimate in classroom success; it was rare that you "got by" with anything where Miss Haldoran was concerned. And she was congratulating herself on her cleverness when she heard Miss Haldoran saying, after a pause, "Since you're so fond of Mark Twain, Miss Kramer, your next assignment will be a full report on his *Innocents Abroad*."

"All of it?" Cheryl gasped. She'd noted the size of the book when cruising the library shelves.

"Why, certainly, my dear. It should be a pleasure."

The rest of the class snickered. Miss Haldoran was a smooth one, all right; there was no mistake about that.

As the afternoon droned on, Cheryl headed for the library during study period in an effort to see how quickly she could skim through Mark Twain. She'd have to take the book home, of course, but she wanted to have a better idea of what lay ahead of her and whether it had pictures that might enliven her task.

She was browsing along the shelves in search of it among fiction under T when she encountered Bill Meyers followed by one of the librarians. He was wheeling a cart of books, and she was giving him instructions as to where to place them in the stacks. It was obvious that the lanky youth was being introduced to a part-time job in the library, and equally obvious to Cheryl that she must spend more of her time here.

The librarian was still hovering about him when Cheryl had to leave for her next class, her original mission postponed. Mark Twain had best wait until tomorrow; it would be an excellent excuse to get into conversation with Bill Meyers by asking him to help her locate it.

"Whatever are you so happy about?" Judy wanted to know as they met to go to their history class. "Anybody'd think you'd found a million dollars or something."

"Tell you later." Even with a best friend, one had to keep some matters private. Judy knew she had a crush on Bill Meyers—they'd talked about it endlessly along with Judy's yen for the editor of the high school paper —but Judy would want to know whether she'd actually talked with Bill Meyers. What she had said, and what he had said. Things like that.

Hurrying on side by side, each absorbed in her own thoughts, they stepped out on the grass to make room for a bevy of Gamma Delts who were bearing down upon them as though they owned the whole sidewalk. Gamma Delts saw no need to step aside for anyone; they could walk five abreast and expect everyone to get out of their way.

"Stuck-ups," Judy muttered. "I wouldn't go to one of their old rushing parties if they asked me."

But Cheryl stared after them enviously. "You'd go, I'll bet." She knew that Judy did not care as deeply about joining a sorority as she did, but what girl could resist an invitation?

"Well, maybe," Judy confessed, "anyway, to see what one's like."

It was hard to concentrate on history with both Bill Meyers and sororities to think about, but Cheryl tried. She'd already gotten herself into enough trouble for one day in American literature not to seek an additional load from the history teacher. Presently, Mr. Sampson was fighting the Civil War all over again, and Cheryl raised her hand to ask why the war had been necessary. Couldn't the North and the South have somehow settled the matter peaceably without killing so many bloody thousands of men?

"Cheryl has asked an excellent question," he said, looking around the class. "Would anyone care to answer it?"

He looked across a forest of upraised hands from students so eager to talk that the classroom rocked with discussion. The dead past was very much alive as the whole subject of war led to the situation in the present day and whether the United States and the Soviet Union would eventually fight.

Without realizing that she was doing so, Cheryl had thrown a conversational bomb. It was with difficulty that Mr. Sampson restored any semblance of order. They seemed far indeed from Gettysburg until he reminded them that war was war whether it was fought with bayonets or with atomic weapons.

"The real question is whether war ever settles anything," he summed it up as the bell rang. "Is there a time in history when war ever has? If you think so, make an outline to prove it."

Like Miss Haldoran, Mr. Sampson had a reputation for giving stiff courses that taught you more than most sophomores were expected to know. He abhorred what he called "lazy minds." At the last school Open House he had told the parents that he was trying to educate "tomorrow's citizens."

Despite Mr. Sampson, the boys in the class didn't act much like citizens of any period, Cheryl thought, as they stampeded to the door as though they'd never heard of "ladies first." Most boys were barbarians, she thought, and Judy agreed with her. Small as she was, Judy stayed close to Cheryl . . . a girl had to watch out lest she be killed in the rush. Boys were savages, and there were few exceptions to this general rule.

By the time classes were over, a light rain was falling. Whatever curl Cheryl had in her hair soon disappeared —she had no scarf to tie over it, and she looked as dank and miserable as she felt when she encountered a group of the Tri Phis. Apparently, they were waiting for rides; but also, quite as obviously, they were inspecting every girl who passed near them.

Cheryl wondered whether any of the other passersby were as self-conscious as she was, as unable to pretend that they didn't care a rubber nickel about how the Tri Phis might rate them. Any girl could be caught in the rain without proper equipment; it wasn't fair of them to decide that she looked like "someone who had been called for and couldn't come," to use one of her grandmother's favorite expressions.

The spring rushing teas could not be far away, and she might very easily not receive a single invitation. Tri Phis, Gamma Delts, and the others might decide that she wasn't worth so much as a cup of tea or an open-faced sandwich. They'd leave her to perish unhonored and unsung among the undistinguished thousands. Competition in this high school was so keen that Cheryl was sure she'd end up as nothing but a picture and a name in the annual if she had no social organization behind her.

An invitation to a rushing tea was the beginning . . . the foot in the door that could lead to what Cheryl pictured as a perfect paradise. Judy and Alicia might claim that they could take sororities or leave them alone, but she often wondered whether they really believed this.

They could be "whistling in the dark."

The test was soon to come; Cheryl could feel it in her bones. One day she'd go home to find an invitation in the mail, or she wouldn't. It would be as simple and as cruel as that.

A white envelope, probably a square one. Maybe two white envelopes. Some girls got invitations to more than one rushing tea on the same afternoon and couldn't decide which to attend. Last semester she had heard them talking about it, but then she hadn't worried. No sophomore in her first semester was ever invited; but, if you weren't asked in your second semester, you could practically count yourself out of the running since juniors were seldom pledged. Desire flamed through Cheryl. It had to be now or never.

6   *By Invitation Only*

It was several days later, when she was standing on the corner waiting for the bus to take her home after school, that she saw Judy and Alicia disappear into the Economy Drug Store. There would always be another bus and shopping around drug stores was always fun, so she decided to join them. If she saw any bargains, she could scrimp on her lunches or bring sandwiches from home to make up the difference; her personal allowance was already overspent.

She found Judy and Alicia poring over the costume

jewelry counter. Judy was trying to choose among the scatter pins—should it be the rhinestone poodle or the spotted enamel deer? Alicia was trying on long dangly earrings which, of course, she'd never wear; they were too sophisticated, but they looked well on her.

Finding a similar pair, Cheryl held them up to her face. She'd read somewhere that long earrings made a plump face look thinner, and maybe they did if you weren't afraid of looking foolish. She always felt silly in anything more than a thin gold chain or a bracelet. What difference did it make if jewelry were half price if it wasn't your type?

The same went for bathing caps out of season, and for the summer bras and shorts that were displayed among all the vitamin pills and the beauty potions that promised you'd look younger in thirty days' time. Why didn't they have a kind of cream that would make you look older overnight? Cheryl could use it.

Her face, as she surveyed it in the drug-store mirror, was positively childish. For a girl as tall as she was— almost five feet seven the last time the gym teacher had measured—having a face like a twelve-year-old was no help to a happy social life. Round chin, full pouting lips, freckles across her nose, and eyes that everyone said were her best beauty feature. Gray sometimes, green at others. If only she were permitted to use eye shadow and mascara as some of the other girls did!

Mother objected even to a beauty foundation under the light coating of powder . . . said it clogged skins and spoiled young complexions. Just as though Cheryl's wasn't bad much of the time even without any cosmetics!

Mother said she was lucky to have an oily skin since it wouldn't be so apt to show wrinkles and other "premature signs of age" later on; but Mother could have it. Mother could have all the problems that went with an oily skin if you didn't scrub it every night—practically right off of your nose.

That was the trouble with having a mother who was also a model; she was an authority on beauty problems, and you couldn't contradict her. Even Mother did not use a great deal of makeup . . . said she'd seen too many skins ruined. When she was around the house in the mornings and on weekends she all but avoided makeup of any kind to give her skin a chance to breathe. Her skin needed a rest as much as she did, she always said. She wore those sloppy slacks of hers because she was tired of being "on stage" elsewhere in the course of her professional life.

Cheryl sighed at the weight of parental authority and went over to examine a basket of lipsticks on sale "two for one." Passion Pink and Rogue Red . . . the names always intrigued her. Orange Kiss, Allure, Temptation . . . if only a lipstick could live up to its name! She decided upon Black Magic, a darker red than she had ever before attempted to wear; it might make her look older. At least it was not what one could call a "wholesome" color like the bright young reds which her mother usually suggested.

Judy and Alicia were more concerned with the blouse

counter where the low prices and the array of prints and colors were tempting them to obey the sign and "refresh your winter-weary wardrobe." Judy was looking through the size eights and tens and Alicia through the twelves, but Cheryl took size fourteen. At the very least. In cheaper blouses, such as these, sixteen would be better. Even to her friends, Cheryl hated to admit that she could wear sixteen, a matronly size if there ever was one. If she didn't do something about her weight, she'd be into the eighteens next.

The Economy Drug Store was a pleasant place to linger when you were reluctant to go along home because you weren't sure what you'd find—or not find—there. Judy and Alicia must feel the same about the rushing-tea invitations as she did, Cheryl thought. She'd never seen either of them take so long to make up their minds about purchases or so slow to drink the cherry phosphates they'd all ordered at the soda fountain.

Any day now, the sorority invitations would be in the mail. Judy and Alicia knew this as well as Cheryl did. They had been talking about it casually in previous weeks, and Cheryl had tried to act the same way. But now that the deadline was upon them, things were different. You didn't want to explain now that the reason you were taking so long about getting home today was because you were afraid to look in the mailbox. If you didn't get an invitation, you'd be embarrassed to admit how much you had counted upon it.

As they took their separate ways, finally, each called, "Give me a ring tonight." They almost always talked with each other sometime during the evening, anyway. Making a point of it could only mean, "Let's check with each other."

Mother was starting dinner when Cheryl arrived, and all the mail was spread across the mantelpiece. She could see, even as she entered, that most of the envelopes were uninteresting oblongs with windows in them that meant bills or ads. But there was a tiny one that just could be. . . .

Cheryl forced herself to make closer inspection. It had already been opened—a birth announcement important only to proud parents announcing the arrival of "Sue Anne weighing in at 7 lbs. 8 oz."

"Nice they've had a baby, I guess," she said to her mother who had come into the living room wearing a flowered smock over her new yellow silk. She was wearing her hair in a new way, swept to the side; she wondered whether Cheryl liked it. Mother was ash-blond this season, and she was going heavy on the mascara for contrast. With her brown eyes, she looked as lovely tonight as she must have been all afternoon. Lovely, if a bit weary. Modeling was hard work.

"Didn't know you were so interested in the mail, Cheryl." Mother might have intended this as an idle remark, but Cheryl bristled. Mother was always reading things into things into THINGS.

"Isn't it all right if I get a letter once in a while?" she snapped.

"Sure, if you've been writing to anybody lately. Your cousin Cora owes you one, doesn't she? You said she'd not answered that last long—"

"Well, for heaven's sake, Mother!" Cheryl stormed off to her room and slammed the door. Didn't a girl have the right to any privacy around here? Parents didn't have to know everything about you, did they? Even to every detail about your correspondence.

She'd been rude to her mother, she knew, and that always made her feel sorry later; but tonight she couldn't help it. If she told Mother about the sorority teas and how desperately eager she was to receive an invitation to at least one of them, Mother would start worrying with her—which would be more than she could bear. There'd be too much explaining to do, and she hadn't the words to express her emotions.

"I wonder what's got into Cheryl." She could hear Mother puzzling aloud to Father when he arrived. Her bedroom was off the living room, and the walls in most of these tract developments were thin. The houses were built more for show than for wear as in the good old days, Grandmother always said with a sniff.

"Nothing, probably, that a good dinner won't fix," was Father's answer.

"Speak for yourself, George." Mother's voice trailed away as she headed back toward the kitchen.

They were having roast pork with mashed potatoes and apple sauce. The broccoli, too, was a favorite of Cheryl's. But tonight she had no appetite. No appetite for food and even less for conversation. Mother was telling about her day and Father was talking about sports, but Cheryl had little to say for herself.

"No more of this good brown gravy?" Mother looked at Cheryl in astonishment when she refused it. "Don't tell me you're taking your weight problem *that* seriously."

"I'm afraid not. It isn't that. It's—well, nothing you can help, and I'm sorry I was cross with you."

"We all have our little moods, don't we?" Thank goodness, Mother was willing to settle for the light touch instead of a scolding.

"Women!" Father shook his head fondly. "You can't live with 'em, and you can't live without 'em."

As her parents bantered across the table, Cheryl felt that some of her earlier tension was leaving her. Perhaps the sororities hadn't sent out their invitations as yet, and everything could still be all right. She began to eat hungrily . . . yes, that probably was the answer. When you were at the dining table with your parents and the FM radio was softly playing soothing music, school and its problems could recede into the background.

She cleared the table and rinsed the plates for the dishwasher, loathe to turn on the angry grind of the garbage disposal and drown out the dreamy strains of the Strauss waltz. "Dum-dum-de-dum-da-dum," she hummed, transported to the Vienna woods and a faraway world of dancing and romance.

"Could you bring yourself to answer the telephone?" Mother called from the family room. "It's always for you at this time of night."

Judy or Alicia must be calling her. Cheryl dried her hands nervously on a towel and picked up the kitchen extension. It was too late now to go to her own room for privacy, and Mother could overhear every word that she said.

"What's new?" Judy didn't sound excited, and Cheryl breathed more easily. Judy was rattling on about the chocolate cream pie they'd had for dinner and how she'd changed the color of her shoes with that new shoe cosmetic. The cat had learned a new trick, Alicia had stopped by. . . . It was one of their garden-variety conversations that could go on for an hour unless parents intervened. Cheryl could hear a roar from Judy's father.

"See you tomorrow." Cheryl put the receiver back on its hook above the cookbooks stacked on her mother's kitchen desk and idly read the note that had been scrawled on a memo pad. "Lunch with Charlotte at the Chanticleer." Charlotte was Ethel's mother, and the date was tomorrow.

Could they be going to talk about anything important —like, well, the Tri Phis? While Cheryl knew that her mother and Mrs. Barnes often met for social chitchat, this timing could be significant. If Mother knew how she was pining to have an invitation to the tea, she'd tell Mrs. Barnes who, in turn, would put pressure on Ethel. But a girl had her pride. . . .

Cheryl didn't want her mother to get into the act. If the members of the sorority didn't consider her good enough material to rate an invitation on her own, she was not about to have Mother scheme to get one for her. In the turmoil of Cheryl's thinking, this much, at least, was clear.

"I declare, Cheryl, there's no living with you." Mother had been expressing herself on this theme, with variations, for a period of days as parental exasperation and Cheryl's impatience grew. It reached its climax one morning when the girl had risen at six thirty to fuss with her hair and still couldn't get it to suit her.

Nothing had gone right, and her mother's helping had only made matters worse. She'd thrown down her brush in a tantrum and sobbed to be let alone. Now, as she looked down at her breakfast cereal, the tears rolled down her cheeks. She'd be tardy, and she'd have to have a note for the principal and likely have to sit in his office all morning. Consternation was piling upon consternation until Mother was so upset that she finally lost patience. "Sometimes I can't stand you, Cheryl."

"And I can't stand either of you today," Father said, loudly regretting that he was not on his way to the office. Wouldn't you know he'd have such a day off?

The least he could do was drive Cheryl to school, for once, was Mother's reply. She wanted him to know that the weight of this chore was always on her and that she was the family martyr.

Father grew calmer as the distance from the house increased. Weaving his way expertly through traffic to get Cheryl to school in time after all, he suggested that Cheryl be more considerate of her mother.

"Maybe that goes for both of us, Dad, don't you think?"

"Could be." He looked down at Cheryl's hand which had crept into his, and squeezed it. "Maybe you'd better get her a little something as a peace offering, h-m-m?"

"Good idea, but what'll I use for money, Pop?"

He reached into his pocket and came out with a five-dollar bill. "If there's any left out of this, better get yourself a wig, huh?"

That was when they both laughed. If she had a wig, there'd be no more fuss about hairdos. She would look around for new heads, too, while she was at it—one for her and one for Father. They both could make use of them, and it would be nice to have a change. Change your head as often as you change your mind.

To avoid more serious topics, Cheryl discussed this with her friends during lunch. Wigs . . . a new head . . . anything that would give you a different personality when you were tired of the old one. When you had to live with yourself year in and year out, you wished for some easy way. . . .

"Maybe we ought to take happiness pills," Judy suggested whimsically. She'd bring a round of them tomorrow from her little sister's toy-doctor kit.

"Better add one for Feeney Chase, too," Cheryl said, noticing out of the corner of her eye that Feeney was bearing down upon them with that earnest look on her face. If Feeney were happier inside of herself, perhaps she wouldn't count so much on the three of them and would let them alone.

But, suddenly, in a flash of honesty Cheryl realized that she was not unlike Feeney. She was as eager in her desire to belong to a sorority as Feeney was to join them at lunch. Everybody wanted to belong to something or somebody, and everyone assumed that someone else had the happiness pill when maybe they didn't at all.

In any case, it was loads more fun to prattle nonsense than to go to class or to wonder why—when she'd made a point of going to the library—she couldn't locate Bill Meyers. She'd hate to ask the librarian whether he was still working there and, if so, what his hours were. The librarian would consider it none of her business.

She'd have to try again this afternoon because she had worked up a whole conversation. She was going to say that she was asking the opinion of leading students on Mark Twain and whether they considered him to be humorous. She was finding *Innocents Abroad* such dull going that she was beginning to wonder, she would say; and, if Bill hadn't read it, so much the better. She could tell him about it.

As her hand touched the crisp bill which her father had given her, she welcomed another diversion. She could wander about the shops after school with the comfortable feeling of riches in her pocket, and buy whatever she thought that her mother would like. It would be a welcome change from the Economy Drug Store.

Alicia thought perfume would be nice, and Judy took the side of lingerie; but Mother had plenty of each. It was the display in the window of a florist shop that arrested them finally and drew them into the store. Pots upon pots of spring flowers . . . hyacinths and tulips and azaleas among branches of what the florist said were flowering peach and almond blossoms, a fairy arch of pink and white overhead.

Except for a few mildewed roses, Mother did not yet have flowers in their yard. This was what she would love. Nothing in a big pot because that would be too heavy to carry, but something special and even spectacular. Mother had a big green vase, and these stocks would be perfect for it . . . fragrant spires of color that were almost a yard long. Spicy rosettes of purple and deep rose and white picked only that morning in gardens that sloped down to the sea, the florist said, approving the freshness of Cheryl's choice and wrapping them in a great cone of green paper.

Everyone on the bus going home exclaimed over her beautiful burden, and several people stopped her on the street to ask whether the Kramers were having a party. Cheryl danced on happily, not bothering to explain. She was anxious to thrust the bouquet into her mother's arms, not only as a peace offering but as an expression of love from her and her father. It was good to have something other to think about than tea-party invitations.

"All this for me?" Mother cradled the giant bouquet.

It was much later when Cheryl discovered the slim white envelope. It was addressed to her in bright blue ink, and it had been postmarked only that morning.

7 *"What Shall I Wear?"*

"You open it, Mom." Cheryl asked, not trusting herself to do so; she could not control the tremble in her
fingers. "See what's in it and—and read it to me."

"I never saw you in such a state, Cheryl. Are you sure
you're all right?" Mother assumed her better-take-your-
temperature expression.

"Just read it, Mom . . . that's all I'm asking. To see
what's inside the envelope."

"Cheryl Kramer is invited to be the guest of Tri Phi
sorority on Sunday, March 10, from three until five

o'clock." Those were the magic words, and Cheryl barely listened to the rest. R.S.V.P. and the address.

She leaped from her chair and whirled her mother about the room in a dance of pure joy. When they both had collapsed on the sofa, Cheryl wondered for the first time about the R.S.V.P. She knew, of course, that it meant that the invitation was supposed to be answered, but what did the initials stand for—actually? She had to understand every momentous phrase.

"It's the French for 'reply, if you please' . . . *'répondez s'il vous plaît.'* Haven't you had that in school?" Mother was often impatient with modern methods of education. "Accept or decline, you know."

Imagine anyone declining when the door to a high school heaven had swung open wide! It was beyond the realm of reason that any girl would not be overjoyed to accept, but Mother thought otherwise. Mrs. Barnes wasn't too keen about Ethel's activities or her general attitude since she had joined the sorority, Mother said. Cheryl would be wise to think it over.

"They don't ask everyone to a rushing tea, Mom. It means you've been specially picked."

"Yes, and a rushing tea doesn't mean that they'll pledge you either, my pet. Never lose sight of that possibility. Don't you think they had sororities when I was in high school?" Mother didn't exactly date from the dark ages. "They didn't call them that—they called them clubs—but it was the very same thing. A lot of girls were hurt by the clubs; but, thank goodness, I wasn't one of them."

Father, when he came home, was equally unenthusiastic. "You don't suppose I needed a sorority to find your mother, do you? I could tell a cute trick the first time I saw her at that football game."

Was he going into that old story again? How he'd been sitting on the bench waiting to be called into the game when Mother had gotten so excited over a touchdown that she'd lost her balance. She'd toppled from the cheering section practically into his lap. Father always ended his account with the same impossible pun, "She fell for me."

Parents never, never understood. They imagined that they did, but they didn't; they judged from the viewpoint of their own high school days. And times had changed. Cheryl was sure that they had changed as much as the clothes in those funny old snapshots. Mother in a beanie hat and some kind of sweater she called a "sloppy Joe," and Father standing beside her in, of all things, a double-breasted suit with wide lapels.

They didn't remember what it was like to go around floating several feet off the ground as you hurried into your room to compare notes with your friends. Thank goodness for her extension telephone and the freedom to flop on her bed while she talked to Judy and Alicia.

The Tri Phis had invited them, also. All three girls were so thrilled that the conversations didn't make sense tonight. You didn't care whether they did or not; you wanted to burble and giggle and generally blow off the steam that had been building up to the explosion point.

"Why don't you give your invitation to your cat?"

Cheryl teased Judy about her pretended lack of interest in sororities. She and Alicia suggested that they all dress alike for the tea and, as on television, bill themselves as a sister act. Nonsense flowed freely until various fathers thundered equal rights to the use of their phones.

"It's getting so our own friends have to reach us by carrier pigeon." Father scowled as Cheryl emerged from her room. "I've had enough of your tying up the phone half the night."

"I'll try to do better, Father dear."

George Kramer eyed her suspiciously. Whenever Cheryl addressed him as "Father" instead of as "Dad" or as "Pop," she was apt to follow it up with a major request.

"I'm afraid I've been a perfect little beast." Cheryl apologized to both of her parents. "I mean for the last week or so."

She had been behaving dreadfully, she knew. She was sorry about it, especially when she might soon be putting them up to a great deal of expense. What with Father and Mother loudly complaining these days about their income tax coming due, this was a poor time of the year for a girl to need a whole new outfit more attractive than any she'd ever before owned. An outfit that, in every detail, had to be absolutely perfect. With Mother and Father not in sympathy with sororities to begin with, she would have to do a top selling job.

Judy and Alicia had a similar problem. Families weren't about to spend a ton of money getting you dressed up for a sorority tea, even though, as the girls saw it, these two hours could be the most important of their lives. Instead, the correct approach must include Easter. Whatever you wore to the tea, they agreed, you should be able to wear also on Easter.

With this in mind, Judy and Alicia came over to spend several afternoons perusing the pages of the fashion magazines so abundant in the Kramer household. Many of them had special sections featuring clothes for the younger set and how they should be worn—with what hats, what shoes, what jewelry. The girls were deciding also upon colors, doing thorough research before the time came to shop. They had to be well equipped to face mothers bent upon bargains and eager to force them into clothes that were cheaper or on sale or marked CLEARANCE.

Because of the casual mode of dress so customary in southern California, not one of the three girls had ever worn a real suit or what, in the fashion magazines, was called a costume ensemble—a dress matching a jacket or coat. Either would be perfect for the tea and for Easter, but either was a far cry from the simple coordinates which presently made up their wardrobes. Blouses and skirts and sweaters and an occasional dress was their sum total thus far. For the tea it would have to be different.

Alicia had found a caption under a page of suits and costumes which read, "Perfect for year-round wear in California." That could be their slogan to convince the most economy-minded of mothers. She had discovered it none too soon.

Because of her modeling, Cheryl's mother was more fashion-conscious than Judy's or Alicia's; but even she wanted to review Cheryl's whole wardrobe before they talked about anything new. Judy had a white sharkskin dress from last summer which her mother insisted was the very thing for the tea. Alicia had a pink knit, and Cheryl a navy blue sheer. Their mothers were alike in wanting them to wear outfits that had lost their original freshness and would need alterations. Mother couldn't understand that . . . you couldn't be smart in last-season's clothes which you'd never liked in the first place.

Both Judy and Alicia still had Christmas money they could use toward new outfits, if worse came to worse, but Cheryl had spent all of hers. Now all she could do was to take a firm stand.

"You're making such a fuss about what you're going to wear that anybody would think you were buying a trousseau," Mother said crossly as Cheryl again scorned the sheer. They'd bought it on sale for their vacation trip to San Francisco, and today Cheryl hated it the more when her mother pointed out that it was slimming.

A fine thing to have a mother who was a model but who sent her daughter to a tea in something she was practically calling a "stylish stout." Cheryl put her indignant thoughts into words that she hoped would sting her mother's vanity, but her mother only laughed.

"You're no credit to me the way you go to school every day, you know."

When you had made Mother laugh, half the battle was won, as Cheryl knew from years of experience.

Laughing, too, she pressed her advantage. Here was Mother's chance to show off for once . . . to have a daughter who looked like a fashion plate.

"Mind you I'm making no promises," Mother said, still laughing as she helped put Cheryl's room back in order. Clothes and petticoats were strewn across the bed, and shoes upon the chairs. "Perhaps I can find something suitable in one of the shows I'm doing. We've got to watch the expense."

"Can't we look in the shops, too, Mom? Maybe up in Los Angeles," Cheryl added hastily. "You always say they have lots of values up there."

"Remind me not to talk so much, will you?" Mother was still in good humor when Father came home.

Cheryl seldom visited Los Angeles and had rarely been in any of the big stores, but Mother knew where to go. She was surprised when they passed through the downtown area without stopping and headed up on Wilshire Boulevard. The shops here were more exclusive and expensive, and she hadn't dreamed that her mother would even consider them. It would be fun to look, anyhow. Mother answered Cheryl's unspoken question as she left the car in a parking lot and led the way toward the door of a handsome marble building with a uniformed attendant.

You could feel how expensive the store was the moment you entered it, breathed the fragrance of rare perfumes, responded to the glitter of the lavish displays. The store had what Cheryl and all her friends called glamour, and the clerks looked as if they were about to snub anyone not dressed in mink. Timidly, Cheryl stayed close to her mother who often modeled in stores of this type and was not a bit overpowered.

As they went to the upper floors and her mother toured expertly from department to department, Cheryl began to wish they'd stayed in Belmont Beach where she belonged. Most of the price tags were exorbitant—higher than any but the rich could afford—and she was seeing nothing she liked. Mother might be enjoying herself on this cruise, but to Cheryl they were wasting time that was precious. Had her mother forgotten that the tea was only a week away, and that this might be their last afternoon to shop?

"Let's go somewhere else, Mom," Cheryl was pleading when Mother met a saleswoman whom she knew and stopped to chat with her.

Cheryl turned away to examine a table loaded with cashmere cardigans in such exquisite spring pastels that the blue bulky she was wearing looked dingy beside them. Dingy and drooping like her spirits. She was not enthusiastic when her mother returned with the bright information that they were going back to the stockroom, whatever that might be. The woman she had met was a clerk in the Young Angeleno Shop and, after her coffee break, would show them a new group of specials.

Cheryl groaned. Mother was bargain hunting again; she should have known it. The suits wouldn't go on sale for several days, Mother continued, but the woman would let them have the benefit of the price ahead of time. "That's what comes of having friends in the business," Mother exulted.

It did, indeed. Mother would see something she liked, at a price that she liked, and Cheryl would have to take that or nothing. If Cheryl refused to cooperate, her mother would be aggrieved and say that was all the thanks she got when she and Father tried to do their very best for her. Cheryl had heard her so often that she knew the exact tones her mother would use.

As Cheryl trailed behind them back to the stockroom, which was going behind-the-scenes, she discovered, she had little hope for success. The clerk was showing them a rack of light-weight wool suits that only faintly resembled what she had set her heart upon in the magazines. Some had short jackets and some skimmed the hips, but they had too many pockets or were over-resplendent with fancy buttons and bows. Mother was commenting that the buttons could be replaced and that the bows could be removed, but Cheryl only half-heard her.

She would rather wear the navy blue sheer than any of these suit specials, she was telling herself, when she glimpsed a green-and-white checked wool in the rack next to them that seemed to be precisely the suit of her dreams.

"Couldn't I try this one on, Mom? Please?" She didn't dare to look at the price tag.

"That's one of our little successes," the saleswoman said pleasantly, holding up the suit. It had a long torso jacket. "Takes a tall girl to wear it. Body-slimming lines, you know. It's the last one in stock."

But Mother was adamant. They could bring the checked suit to the fitting room if they liked, but it would have to be accompanied by several of the specials which must be Cheryl's first consideration.

"Any one of them will do very well." Mother considered Cheryl's varying reflections in the full-length mirrors of a room which had blond wood and bright leather-covered chairs.

"But they're not me," Cheryl protested. "I don't feel right in them. Honestly, I don't."

"She has your fashion sense," the clerk said, flattering Mother and at length persuading her to let Cheryl try on the outfit she cherished.

"It's 'way too expensive." Mother prepared not to like it.

As Cheryl slipped into the soft beautiful wool, amply cut so that it did not pull at her anywhere, she knew that this was *her suit*. Some clothes spoke to you warmly, and others left you quite cold. There was no explaining exactly why this could happen; it was something that you knew inside of yourself.

The jacket fell below her hips and shaped her figure in exactly the right places. The skirt had an easy fullness. It was a suit that would not require a single alteration, and the green of the check brought out the green of her eyes.

"Absolutely perfect," the saleswoman crooned over her.

Mother grudgingly agreed; it was perfect from every angle except for the price. "I don't pay nearly as much as this for my own clothes. My husband would have a fit if I . . ." her voice trailed off, hesitant.

"Perhaps I can get you some reduction since it's the last one we have." The saleswoman hurried away to talk to the buyer. Cheryl, alone with her mother, pleaded her case. She'd wear her last year's bathing suit . . . she'd not ask for any new playclothes this year . . . she'd learn to knit and make her own sweaters.

"You mean that, if I buy you this suit, I'll practically be saving money in the end?" Mother's eyes glinted with humor as Cheryl outlined her forthcoming thrift. She wouldn't ask for another single thing all year; the suit was all that she wanted.

"Besides a few little things like the accessories to go with it," Mother reminded her, enumerating hat and blouse, shoes, gloves, and purse.

"W-ell, yes," Cheryl admitted and hastily pointed out that even the suit specials would require similar additions.

"Wish I'd never heard of sororities." Mother turned to the saleswoman who returned with the beaming announcement of a slight savings in price. "That the best you can do?"

"Please, Mom, please." Cheryl's eyes darkened, sure signs of approaching storm. It was horrid to be so helpless, always to have so little money of your own to spend.

"Perhaps she can fit it into her clothes allowance," the saleswoman said, assuming that all girls were so lucky as to have generous ones.

"I suppose it *is* a good buy for a suit of this quality."

Mother examined the silk lining again and reluctantly took out her checkbook.

Cheryl waited at the service desk while her precious package was wrapped, savoring the rustle of the tissue paper placed between the folds of the lovely fabric, relishing the smart brown-and-white striped box and the golden cord being tied around it with a loop to make it easy for her to carry it.

She swung proudly through the store after Mother, who said they'd best hurry before Cheryl saw something else that she couldn't resist. Lucky it was almost closing time. But it was Mother who slowed down at the Hat Bar to admire the display of Easter bonnets. She almost picked one out for herself. Almost, but not quite. She was too tired to make a sensible choice, she said, either for her or for Cheryl. Besides, there was no point in overwhelming Father all at once with too many boxes from the Boulevard.

On the Saturday night before the tea, Cheryl staged a dress rehearsal. Grandmother had been there for dinner with an aunt from out of town. And, as Cheryl went into her room to dress in a flurry of excitement, Father jokingly asked what record she wanted him to put on the player in time for her fashion show.

She needed more practice walking in high heels, Cheryl decided, slipping into the bone-colored pumps which she and Mother had found in a local shoe store, along with a bag to match it. She hadn't cared for the white sailor hat which Mother had suggested, and they had compromised on a deep-crowned, straw cloche. The white frilly blouse and white gloves completed a costume that was smarter because they'd used two colors for the accessories, Mother explained. This was the latest thing to do.

Father whistled with admiration when she appeared, and Mother and her aunt glowed, but Grandmother pursed up her lips. They had probably spent too much for such an outfit . . . it was too sophisticated for a girl of fifteen . . . and, as usual, they were spoiling her. "Fine feathers do not make fine birds." Grandmother summed up the matter as Cheryl pranced.

"But they can make you feel simply ducky." Cheryl blew a kiss in her grandmother's direction. She could not be cross with anyone tonight.

8 *Admirable Drive*

The Tri Phi tea was to be held at the home of one of the senior girls whose family was reputed to have a great deal of money. As the fateful hour approached, Cheryl was beginning to have stage fright. Suppose her suit didn't look as well on her as she thought that it did. Suppose she couldn't think of anything to say. Suppose a thousand things went wrong—like breaking one of these slim narrow heels that she'd already caught in a scatter rug. She had thought that her nail polish was precisely the shade of her lipstick; but now, as she noted a slight variation, she wondered whether others would notice.

"Really, Cheryl, you're getting yourself into a dither over nothing." Mother was trying to calm her. "If the color of your lipstick is all that matters with the Tri Phis, you're well out of such an organization."

With all the feminine flurry in the household, Father had taken himself off to play tennis. It was getting on his nerves, he said, and it was more than a mere man could stand. But he promised to return in plenty of time to drive Cheryl and her friends to the party. "I'd never dare show my face around here again if I didn't."

As Mother worked expertly over Cheryl's makeup, allowing her more today than was customary, Cheryl began to emerge as a girl who scarcely recognized herself. Darker powder with highlights on the cheekbones minimized the plump outlines of her face; the mascara and green eye shadow, used with a light but telling touch, made her eyes sparkle like emeralds. She looked years older—not like a high school girl at all, but like a woman of the world. Now if she could only live up to her appearance!

She moved about in an aura of sophisticated fragrance . . . Mother's bath oil and perfume and skin sachet . . . with the satin of a beautiful slip falling about her in clinging, caressing folds. Mother wanted her to get dressed in time to pose for several snapshots in color to preserve the memory of an occasion that neither of them was likely to forget.

And then there was nothing to do but wait for her

father. Cheryl looked anxiously at the clock, remembering that he sometimes forgot about time when he was playing tennis. The set could be tied, and he would be late.

"I declare, you're just like your grandmother," Mother exclaimed, as Cheryl sat beside the window and worried.

"Hope I don't look like her." Cheryl raised her head so that Mother could decide for the fifth time how much of her hair should show beneath the snowy-white cloche. A little here . . . more there . . . enough to soften the outlines. It was more youthful worn farther back on the head, Mother decided, moving it an inch or two and standing back to admire the effect.

"I never saw you look better, Cheryl." Mother was finally satisfied. "If that's any help to you. Sure you have a good handkerchief?" She checked last-minute details.

Whatever had happened to Father? He could have had a flat tire or run out of gas. Judy and Alicia had both called several times to ask what was delaying them before Father appeared. He was famished, he said, and he wouldn't stir another foot unless he had something to eat.

Cheryl wailed while Mother prepared a cheese sandwich which she thrust into his pocket. "Better eat it on the way," she advised. "Your daughter's about to have a nervous breakdown."

Father could at least have washed his car, Cheryl thought, settling in the front seat and wishing she had done it herself. Judy and Alicia would think it was as dirty inside as out, and not want to sit in it for fear of spoiling their clothes. The Tri Phis might notice how dusty it was and. . . . A dozen thoughts flashed through Cheryl's overanxious mind as she directed her father to the homes of her friends. By this time, they were probably pacing up and down, and she couldn't blame them. Fathers could be so very exasperating!

Judy ran down her driveway dressed in the navy bolero suit with the polka-dotted blouse and red hat she had described so minutely. Alicia was standing at the curb wearing a smartly tailored gray flannel suit with yellow accessories. Cheryl had heard about the yellow. It had been a family battle between yellow and white (goes with everything), and Alicia must have won it yesterday.

"And now where do you three glamorous creatures want me to take you?" Father cast an approving masculine glance over his passengers.

Cheryl had written down the address—1154 Admirable Drive—but Father had never heard of the street. None of the girls had thought to ask how to find it. As Father consulted a street map, he could see difficulties ahead.

Admirable Drive was one of those jumpy streets which, like so many in Belmont Beach, ran a little way and then stopped at a dead end to continue blocks later. You had to follow many a devious turn until you could discover it again, and the very thought of this made Mr. Kramer cross. The least the girls could have done was to get adequate directions. That wasn't too much to ask, was it? Father glared at them.

As they pursued the bits and pieces of Admirable Drive, the way led them through an area dotted with oil derricks where pumps that looked like crouching grasshoppers bobbed their heads ceaselessly. The stench of oil being drawn from subterranean pools filled the air, and the girls giggled nervously.

While their hostess for the afternoon might be rich because her family owned oil wells, it was far from likely that they lived among them. But Mr. Kramer failed to see the humor of the situation. He was going all around Robin Hood's barn and back, and he had other things to do with his time.

"It can't be much farther, Dad," Cheryl said to encourage him as Alicia glanced at her wristwatch. They were already almost an hour late, but maybe that didn't matter so much when you were bound for a tea, Alicia offered. She expressed a hope that the others did not feel. You didn't sit down at a table at a tea . . . you didn't keep others waiting as at a dinner. But still, if you were invited from three until five, you ought to have been there.

"I couldn't think of anything to say for two hours anyway," Alicia said, taking an optimistic view.

When at length they came to a part of Admirable Drive that looked more promising, they found the number they sought inscribed in bronze upon two gateposts so imposing that Father wryly insisted they must mark a cemetery entrance. Which was all that he needed. . . .

They turned in to follow a road that circled through

what apparently was a family estate. Handsome houses were erected along it, and it had its own private golf course.

"Looks like you've got yourself a millionaire," Mr. Kramer said, still grumbling as they pressed on to discover a home that yielded signs of a party. Most presented a bland and unwelcoming exterior to the outside world, but on ahead they could see parked cars and people flowing in and out through the lines of a carefully clipped hedge.

As they came closer, they could recognize some of the girls who were being escorted to the door of a Georgian brick house by anxious fathers. Cheryl hoped her parent would not be similarly gracious; he was still dressed in old tennis shorts.

But she needn't have worried. He appeared only too glad to be rid of his cargo, and he drove off with a shout that Cheryl hoped against hope did not carry as far as the house. What he had cried was, "Best of luck, girls. Do or die!"

As Cheryl walked toward the house, she could feel herself trembling. Judy dropped one of her gloves out of nervousness. Only Alicia appeared calm.

"So nice of you to come." Patsy Moore, their hostess, met them at the door accompanied by her mother who was wearing one of those long slim gowns in a flowered silk print that Cheryl's mother would admire.

"It's a pleasure, I'm sure," Alicia murmured, and Cheryl took her cue from her friend.

Left to herself, she might have blurted out something

like "I've been counting on it," or "I couldn't wait," or something equally frank but inappropriate. She must stick close to Alicia who had a poise that Cheryl was beginning to appreciate.

"Do sign our guest book, won't you?" Patsy led the way to a hall table flanked by antique mirrors that made you look all squiggly and distorted. It was the way Cheryl was starting to feel as she prepared to enter the crowded room beyond.

Everyone was chatting to everyone else and balancing delicate teacups in one hand while they used the other for gestures. Not one of them seemed overawed by the formality and elegance of a room that reminded Cheryl of the lobby of some fine hotel.

When several of the other girls took over from Patsy to escort them about, Cheryl found herself separated from Alicia and completely on her own. It was Sue Shaw who had chosen Cheryl as her responsibility, and Sue Shaw, doubtless, who had suggested that she be invited. Sue had the school locker next to hers, and they had become the sort of friends who loan each other lunch money and lipsticks. She liked Sue, who never put on airs until today when everyone seemed strange.

Certainly her invitation had not come through Ethel Barnes who was looking at her from across the room but had made no move to welcome her. Ethel was staring her up and down in a way that transfixed Cheryl until she realized why this was. They were both wearing the same suit, but it looked so different on Ethel that she had not, at first, noticed that the suits were identical.

The long jacket made Ethel look so short that it did not become her; she must have chosen it because it was in the height of fashion, regardless of whether it suited her.

Cheryl was of a height that could carry it off, and Ethel must be furious. Who was Cheryl Kramer to afford so expensive a suit, and then look better in it than she did? No wonder those button eyes of Ethel's were snapping with anger.

Sue Shaw had noticed this bit of byplay, and she laughed. "Ethel doesn't like anyone else to get ahead of her, does she? The suit's marvelous on you," she added in a tone that implied she enjoyed seeing Ethel's nose out of joint.

Clearly, she was not overfond of Ethel either. Belonging to a sorority did not mean that you had to regard every member of it with sisterly affection. Cheryl sensed a firm ally in Sue; maybe she'd want her to become a Tri Phi in order to spite Ethel, if for no other reason.

However she made the break into Tri Phi, Cheryl was surer than ever that she wanted to do it. These girls around her seemed to have all the answers . . . in poise and in polish, in light and easy small talk. Given the chance, some of all this might rub off on her, and Cheryl could use it.

Besides, it would be glamorous to know girls as rich as Patsy. Why she attended a public high school was a mystery that only added to her charm in Cheryl's eyes. Some said her family had taken her out of a finishing school in the East because they wanted to keep closer tabs. She was wild, these presumed authorities said, and had tried to elope. Her family tried to intercept letters from some boy in Switzerland because they wanted to break up the romance. Brightly colored rumors about Patsy had drifted about Hunterford High, and Cheryl had devoured them.

Now that she was seeing for herself the setting in which Patsy lived, the stories glowed even more rosily. Cheryl had never before been in so wealthy a home, nor had she ever seen so magnificent a silver tea service as the one that graced the dining-room table. The lace cloth was laden with dainty tea cakes frosted in pastels with rose-buds . . . open-faced sandwiches offered tiny black dots that must be caviar . . . there were spreads of every imaginable kind. One could have punch instead of tea—punch in tall frosted glasses from a bowl in which an ice swan floated beside a centerpiece of green orchids and ivory white camellias.

Cheryl was dazzled by the whole effect, but the Tri Phis seemed to accept it as a matter of course. Many of the girls had parents no wealthier than Cheryl's—Ethel Barnes, for one, and a girl whose name she could not recall but who was pouring tea and asking in a stilted voice whether cream or lemon was preferred. Cheryl had seen this girl's lingerie sometimes when she dressed for gym, and it often was ragged. Yet anyone watching her performance now would assume that she had been born to the purple.

If the truth were known, there must be many others like her moving from drawing room to library to an indoor-outdoor pool paved in white marble with a roof over it that Sue said could be closed for winter swimming. Pools were no novelty to Cheryl—lots of tract houses had them—but none was as large as this or with a cocktail bar at one end and, at the other, a conservatory filled with exotic plants and the brilliant flash of tropical birds flitting among the flowers and the lush green foliage.

"Did you ever swim here?" she asked Sue in a voice filled with admiration.

"Oh, sure, when we have slumber parties here." Sue spoke as though the Tri Phis often gathered at the Moores'.

It was hard to imagine girls in pajamas flitting informally through a house of this type or making late snacks and messing around in the kitchen. To Cheryl it seemed a showplace to be looked at rather than lived in, but she supposed the Tri Phis got used to it.

"Mrs. Moore likes to have us come here." Sue answered Cheryl's unspoken question. "Says it warms the place up and makes Patsy more contented."

She introduced Cheryl to three Tri Phis whom she had seen around school and then to several who looked to be well up in their twenties but who were wearing the sorority pin. "Have to impress our alumnae, you know," Sue said gaily and then—as though to cover Cheryl's halting responses and perhaps to bolster her against later opposition from Ethel—added, "This girl's a brain. She gets A in science."

"What a beautiful suit," one of them remarked graciously, "and you wear it so well. Perfect accessories."

Cheryl wanted to explain that her mother was a model and deserved most of the credit, but then she thought better of it. They wouldn't be interested in part of her life history . . . they might put her down as naive. All she could think of to say was, "Thank you very much," and "I like your suit, too."

Her words sounded like so many stones plunked down in the midst of light conversation that, like bubbles, drifted past and ignored her. All she could do was to stand there and smile. Perhaps that was all that was expected of a rushee, but she felt that more was required.

With the smile still frozen on her face, she followed Sue back inside and to more introductions which she stiffly acknowledged. Judy appeared to be enjoying herself, as did Alicia, but Cheryl could not relax and act natural. There seemed so little to say, really, except, "Isn't it a gorgeous afternoon?" And there seemed so little to do except to go back to the dining room for more cakes and more punch.

On the second of these excursions, her purse swung against her glass. In an effort to steady it, half the contents was spilled. As one of the maids in attendance rushed to mop up the carpet, Mrs. Moore kindly observed that it hadn't done the slightest harm and not to worry, but Cheryl was not reassured. Several Tri Phis had observed her mishap, and they were not apt to think kindly about a girl who could not so much as manage a glass without making a mess with it. The word would get around.

As Mrs. Moore drew her over to the window seat to

engage in conversation, she wished that a few of the girls had half this older woman's talent for putting you at your ease. She found herself talking readily to Mrs. Moore, admiring her dress and telling about Mother whom Mrs. Moore was sure she'd seen in many a fashion show. "I don't look much like her, I'm afraid." Cheryl sighed.

"You've a lot of growing up to do, and don't try to hurry it up too fast." A cloud came over Mrs. Moore's face as she glanced at her own daughter who was laughing so shrilly and so frequently that it seemed artificial. "That's the trouble with a lot of you girls these days. You want to grow up too fast."

Ethel Barnes had come into the room and, seeing that Mrs. Moore was paying marked attention to Cheryl, walked over to join them. "Isn't it a scream to be look-alikes?" she asked, indicating their suits. "Cheryl and I have known each other for years, but I didn't know we thought alike, too."

"Happens all the time. I wouldn't let it bother me." Mrs. Moore had detected the edge in Ethel's tone and was putting her in her place. "Have you met all the girls?" She turned again to Cheryl and, linking arms with her, strolled through the various rooms.

Her charm and thoughtfulness were rapidly restoring Cheryl's self-confidence, and she was soon able to talk more spontaneously. Several of the girls to whom Mrs. Moore introduced her remarked, "We must get to know each other better." That must mean they liked her enough to want her in Tri Phi, Cheryl thought. Her spirits rose steadily as the tea party drew to a close. It was nearly six o'clock, but everyone seemed reluctant to leave.

Even Patsy Moore took new interest in Cheryl and asked whether she'd care to have a look at her room. "Oh, yes," Cheryl breathed. "I'm sure it's just lovely."

She looked at the coverlet tossed with taffeta pillows in every shade of the rainbow and strewn with flowers that matched those on the drapes and even on the towels in the dainty pink bathroom. Bottles of perfume in every size and shape stacked a dressing table whose focal point was a photograph in a wide silver frame. Coming closer to admire the portrait of a youth whose hair fell in waves above a high forehead and burning dark eyes, Cheryl read the inscription upon it, "To the love of my life from Nicky." Patsy was, indeed, a girl who had everything.

As Cheryl bade the Moores a lingering good-bye, she could truly say now that she had had a wonderful time. Alicia's father had arrived to pick them up and Alicia was plucking at her sleeve to get her to hurry, but she wanted to do more than bid them a polite and perfunctory farewell.

"I'm counting upon seeing you again," Mrs. Moore called to her as she followed Alicia down the sidewalk.

"So am I." Cheryl waved back, and then wondered whether that had sounded too bold. She tossed off the self-doubt that swept over her momentarily and jumped gaily into the car.

9 *S-Day*

"I thought the Moores were going to feed you," Father remarked as Cheryl asked for another helping of potatoes and pot roast. She had been too excited to eat much for lunch, and now she was starving. "From the looks of their place, they could afford it."

A few bits of party food were nothing like dinner. Didn't Father know that? You didn't go to a rushing tea for the sole purpose of eating. Between mouthfuls, she was giving her mother a play-by-play description of her afternoon.

"Sounds like a tempest in a teapot," Father said, scoffing at a conversation that, to him, seemed utterly frivolous.

"Hush, dear, it's important to Cheryl." Mother brushed him aside to give full attention to what Mrs. Moore had worn and what she'd said.

"High society . . . too high for a daughter of mine." Father refused to be ignored.

The Tri Phis weren't all like that, Cheryl explained, with all the patience she could manage. They were the biggest sorority in school, but you didn't have to have loads of money to join. They voted on you, and the sort of person you were made all the difference.

"Oh, is that so? First time I ever heard of a snob group deciding anything on merit." Father banged his fist on the table. "They're a snob group, I tell you. A lot of little people who think they're big when they vote against you because they don't like the shape of your nose."

"Or *for* you, Dad. Don't you know how much I want to belong?" Cheryl looked at him earnestly. "I never wanted anything so much in all of my life."

"When do they vote, chick?" Father softened.

"Sometime this week, I guess. I don't know for sure when they send out the bids. All the sororities had their rushing parties today."

"That figures," Father said indignantly. "Dozens of girls put on the rack all at once. Thought this was supposed to be a civilized country."

Tactfully, Mother changed the subject. She had

begun to wonder, she said, about spring renovation, and whether Father was going to alter the kitchen colors. Father was trying to take all the fun out of the tea for Cheryl, and she wasn't about to permit this. The drapes in the living room would do for another year, she said, but Father would have to wash down the walls.

"Always another job for me when I want to go fishing." Father groaned. "We had a good time that day, didn't we, Cheryl?"

"Yes, I guess so." The thought of Peter Guinness flashed into her mind. Peter and the whales. Maybe, by now, he'd been swallowed.

She felt tired suddenly, and talked-out, but it was a contented kind of tiredness. She had done her best, and the glow of elation still remained with her. Therefore, she did not object when her mother suggested that she go directly to bed. "It's been a hard day, dear, and you need your rest."

"How about the dishes?"

"I'll do them for once, but don't make it a habit." Mother came into the bedroom to make sure that she put her precious suit in a garment bag instead of tossing it over a chair. As though she would be so careless with it . . . really!

"Thanks for getting it for me, Mom. Thanks for everything." She gave her mother a hug before she began a search for pajamas.

"Probably under the bed, as usual." Mother frowned as she knelt down to fish them out for her and discover what else might be contained in this catchall. "Honestly,

Cheryl!" she scolded, as she came out with an odd bedroom slipper, stray nylons, and two pairs of ankle socks.

"No night for a lecture, please, Mom," Cheryl protested sleepily, wondering whether Patsy Moore had a
maid to pick up after her.

Cheryl kept her glow all through Monday; but by
Tuesday she was nervous, as were Judy and Alicia.
Countless others were in a similar predicament, and
only sophomores like Feeney Case were lighthearted
and with little to worry them. They hadn't been asked
to anyone's tea, and they weren't sitting on tenterhooks.
Feeney's prattle was maddening as she told the plot of a
movie she'd seen and wanted to know what television
shows they'd watched last night and whether she should
wear her hair with a bandeau. As though, at a time like
this, trivial things mattered. Really, Feeney could be
impossible!

But she was easier to face than Sue Shaw and other
Tri Phis one encountered, wondering what their decision might be. You imagined that one was warm toward
you, another cold; then you tried to tell yourself that,
whichever it was, you had nothing to fear. Different
girls had different personalities . . . that was all it could
possibly be.

While the sororities were not officially recognized by
the school, they had developed a pattern of their own
and acted together. They had their rushing parties on
the same day so that it was difficult for a girl to attend
more than one. If she were so fortunate as to receive

several invitations, she had to choose between them. The teas were the first hurdle. The second was the conclaves that followed them when the sororities met to pick you to pieces and then, maybe, put you back together again in a shape to be pledged.

Alicia knew all about this from her mother who had herself been a sorority girl. While it might seem unjust to judge a girl by the way she appeared at only one party, that was the procedure at Hunterford High. Other schools might have other approaches; and, of course, colleges and universities were quite another matter.

On Wednesday afternoon, a rumor began circulating around school that tonight was the night. It was what had come to be called "S-Day," which meant that sometime during the evening a group of girls would call at your house, give you your bid, and carry you away to be pledged. If you were among the lucky ones, that is . . . the ones who remained after the final screening took place.

Cheryl had forgotten all about that funny old wishing ring which had been tumbling about in the bottom of her purse, but now was the time to retrieve it. The ring was too large to fit on any but her index finger. It was conspicuous there, but this afternoon she didn't care. She would use a rabbit's foot and a four-leaf clover, too, if she had them. One might pretend that such luck charms were silly and superstitious, but what harm was there in taking all the precautions? She would avoid walking under any ladders on her way home from school, and she hoped she wouldn't meet any black cats.

Judy said she was going to clean her room after school just to keep herself occupied, and Alicia had saved up a load of washing to do. Cheryl thought perhaps she could finish the job of clearing out the garage which her father had started. You couldn't sit around merely waiting, or you'd drive yourself crazy.

Whatever happened, the three of them would stick together. They made a solemn vow there in the little grove of eucalyptus trees where the long branches swept almost to the ground and gave a bit of privacy from all the campus rush. When Judy suggested that they might make the vow more binding by writing it upon a piece of paper and pricking their fingers to seal it with blood, they giggled hysterically. That would be going too far, but it was a relief to be able to laugh.

"One for all and all for one," Alicia said, remembering *The Three Musketeers* which she had recently read. It seemed a good note on which to go their separate ways to await whatever the night might hold for each of them.

Cheryl decided to walk today, instead of taking the bus. It was such a lovely spring afternoon that she hated the thought of going inside for so much as a minute. The garage job could wait until Saturday.

It was always like this in southern California after a rain. This rain had stopped in the early hours of the morning; it had swept flowers from the trees to sprinkle the ground with the fuzzy yellow balls of the acacia and the fragrant waxen petals of what went by the name of mock orange. In bloom everywhere was the bird-of-paradise—a flower that didn't look much like a flower but more like a saucy bird with an orange crest. Children were making mud-pies and castles and sailing leaf boats and twigs in the streams which still ran toward the gutters. Listening to the *slap-slap* of jumping ropes, Cheryl longed to forget her fifteen years and leap into "salt, vinegar, mustard, cider, pepper. . . ."

Rain came so seldom here that the day following a downfall seemed almost like a holiday decked out with fresh-washed flowers and the sparkle of leaves. You could not feel dispirited or anxious as you walked through such a day, leaving your troubles behind you to be picked up all too soon. Now Cheryl felt like dancing to the tinkling music of the ice-cream man's cart . . . now she wanted to be a kite flying high in the sky.

"Why so cheerful? Has anything happened?" Mother looked up as Cheryl came whistling through the door and banged down her schoolbooks.

"Nothing yet, Mom, but I feel so good I'm sure that it will." Cheryl explained about "S-Day," and her mother agreed that it might be a good idea to eat early tonight.

"Wouldn't want the Tri Phis to catch me with egg on my face." Cheryl wondered aloud whether she should change now or later.

"Speaking of eggs, if I were you I wouldn't count my chickens before they are hatched."

"Honestly, Mom, you sound exactly like Grandmother." Cheryl started off for her room with an indignant swish of her skirt and then returned to ask for the loan of her mother's new nail polish. "No harm trying to look decent, is there?"

"No, dear, no harm at all." Mother looked at Cheryl with a tenderness that her daughter did not relish. She needed to have Mother share her confidence, not act as though she might need comforting.

She was on the phone with Judy and Alicia until almost dinnertime when Mother reminded her that the Tri Phis might call first before they came. With the lines tied up, how could any one of them be reached? As Cheryl replaced the instrument upon its hook, she again twirled the wishing ring and pressed upon it hard.

When Mother placed a plate of food in front of her and said she herself would wait for Father, Cheryl again surprised the tender look. Neither she nor Mother had anything at all to worry about, she reassured herself, eating with hearty appetite. Probably, this time around, the Tri Phis would not serve you refreshments.

She looked out into the early dusk and wondered exactly when they'd arrive and who would come for her. She could see the crescent of the new moon with one star beside it; and, going out on the lawn into the faint pink afterglow of the sunset, she raised her head to the heavens.

"Star-bright, star-light, first star I've seen tonight. Wish I may, wish I might, have the wish I wish tonight." She added in a fervent whisper, "Please, star, this one time for sure. It's awfully, awfully special."

When a car slowed down in front of the house and all but stopped, she sucked in her breath. The driver

was a man, possibly one of the fathers. But she could
also see a blur of faces peering through the window glass
and some of the heads were fluffy-haired. It could be a
contingent of Tri Phis. But, as the car passed along
down the street, she told herself that she was foolish to
expect them so early in the evening. No . . . they would
come later.

She went back into the house and tried to concentrate
on *Innocents Abroad,* but Mark Twain was particularly
unfunny tonight. Miss Haldoran had given her a time-
extension on her report. She was close to the end of this
account of the author's travels, but it had been a long
and largely tedious journey. The book had been written
almost a hundred years ago, and that could be part of
the trouble. Besides, it ran into hundreds of pages, and
she liked books to be shorter and quicker.

Short and quick, like the running of footsteps up the
walk toward their door. Cheryl had it open before anyone could knock, and faced a grade school girl from one
of the houses several doors away whose mother wanted
to borrow two cupfuls of sugar.

"Oh." Cheryl returned to her reading, but soon she
was turning the pages with unseeing eyes. Her ears were
alert to the slightest sound along the street, and soon she
put the book down altogether to watch for the beam of
car headlights along the curb or turning into their driveway. She had asked Father to put their own car in the
garage to leave plenty of room, just in case, and now all
was ready and waiting, even to the light switched on
above their front door.

When the phone rang, she ran to answer it with a voice that faintly managed, "Hello." It was a cousin on Mother's side of the family who had dropped into town and wanted to spend the evening with them. Cheryl was grateful when Mother suggested to her that another night would fit better into their plans.

Unexpected company was not welcome tonight, especially when it took the form of Cousin Dorothy. She went to college in northern California and was so popular she was always being voted queen of this or that campus event. Dorothy was the sort of girl who'd likely never had to worry even in high school; the sororities must have pursued her. Thus, she was the very last person with whom one would wish to share the vigil of these minutes that were dragging slowly into hours.

Had Judy said she'd call when she had any news? Had Alicia? Or wouldn't there be time once the Tri Phis appeared? They had talked so much about it that Cheryl couldn't remember what they'd finally decided. Besides, what difference did it make who called whom or when? As the hands of Mother's modern clock over the mantelpiece finally got around to eight o'clock, she could no longer contain her impatience.

Dialing Alicia, she talked only to a small brother who said with maddening vagueness that his sister had gone away somewhere. No, his mother wasn't around . . . no, he didn't know where his daddy was. His voice trailed away, and she could hear only the sound of the television set.

She'd have to talk to Judy! The Tri Phis must have

picked up Alicia first, and Judy would be next on their list. When Judy's mother answered the phone, her heart sank. Yes, the Tri Phis had come for Judy a little while ago; they'd put a chain around her neck and led her away to be pledged.

"What kind of chain?" Cheryl asked as though it could possibly matter. It had been a brass chain decked with flowers, and Alicia had been with them.

"I wouldn't worry if I were you, my dear," Mrs. Adams said kindly. "You live quite a way from here, and from what they said I gather that there were quite a few groups. It's probably taking them longer to get to your house. They'll be there any minute. You'll see."

"Yes, I'll wait and see." She thanked Judy's mother and put the receiver back on its hook. Yes, the Tri Phis ought to be here any time now. Perhaps they had gotten lost . . . didn't know their way around Canterbury Knolls. Mrs. Adams had said that there were several cars of them cruising around in the night with these symbolic chains, and Judy and Alicia might not be aboard to direct the one that was heading this way.

She was glad she had put on a fresh blouse. Now she went into her bathroom to renew the color she had chewed from her lips, and run a comb through hair that her nervous hands had mussed. Under the bright lights, she was pale as a ghost.

She picked up the knitting she had started as a result of the spring economy drive that had been part of her bargain with Mother, and went through several rows of the practice sample which the woman at the yarn shop advised. Anything was better than standing at the window and watching for headlights, but soon she was dropping stitches in such numbers that she put the sample aside. She could not concentrate; she could think of nothing save where the Tri Phis were at this minute. Should she act surprised when they came and, if so, how? What pose should she take?

"Can't you light anywhere, Cheryl? You're driving me crazy," Father said as she crisscrossed from living room to family room to kitchen and back again. "Sit down somewhere, will you?"

She went out into the yard, then, to check on the cars. If one of them stopped, she'd duck into the shrubbery so the occupants wouldn't see her and run to the back door of the house.

It felt better to be outside here with the cool fresh air on her face and, overhead somewhere, the star upon which she had wished. You didn't have to watch the clock out here or look at the silent telephone. You didn't feel quite so much like crying when you were out alone with the night.

10   *The Dam Breaks*

You had to hold yourself together somehow. You had to be able to greet the Tri Phis with a smile on your face and pretend you hadn't been waiting hours for them to come and enslave you. Which must be what the chain signified—the Sorority Chain Gang.

"No point in your catching pneumonia, is there?" It was Father who came out to look for her finally and bring her shivering back into the house.

"They'll be along soon, dear." Mother fluttered about her with hot cocoa and cake, while Father looked at the clock and found it wise to say nothing.

"Perhaps if you should start getting ready for bed, darling." Mother was busy with suggestions. "Or take a bath or—I always wash my hair when I'm expecting something to happen. And then it does—spang in the middle of whatever I'm—"

Suddenly Cheryl was in her mother's arms, sobbing out her heart. There was no use pretending any longer. The Tri Phis had discarded her. Mother's tears mingled with hers, while Father watched the two of them helplessly as though he would do anything he could to remedy the situation but knew it was beyond a mere male.

"I don't have a b-boyfriend. I d-don't have a s-sorority. I don't h-have anything." Cheryl wailed in a voice that was high with hysteria.

"You have us, chick." Father sat down in his favorite armchair and drew Cheryl into his lap. "There, there now." He was trying to soothe her as he had done when she was a much smaller girl.

Mother paced near them, indignantly giving voice to her opinion of sororities or of any group that had such power to hurt. She'd warned Cheryl that she might be disappointed; she'd tried to prepare her. "You can't count on anything in this life, and the sooner you learn it the better." She said it with such bitterness that her husband looked at her in astonishment.

"I don't mean you, George. You're the one person who has never let me down. Or let Cheryl down." Mother's tears poured afresh over the affront to her child. It was far more painful than any such slight to herself.

With two hysterical females on his hands, Father stood up straight and tall and ordered them both off to bed. Things always looked worse at night than in the morning, he said, and a good night's sleep never hurt anyone. With this, he went off to the kitchen to prepare them a nightcap. Warm milk always put you to sleep.

When he came into Cheryl's room with her cup to be sure that she was well tucked away, he arranged the pillows about her with clumsy solicitude. "Want me to tell you the story of The Three Bears the way I used to do?"

"Thanks for being so nice to me, Pop." Cheryl pressed her tear-stained cheek against his hand.

Switching out the light on her headboard, she sobbed into her pillow and, falling at length into fitful dreams, called out in her sleep. So Mother said, coming in to console her. Life wasn't over by any means, and she had lots of fun to look forward to. . . .

"Doing what?" Cheryl cried out in despair. It wasn't any help to have Mother remind her that there must be dozens of other girls tonight who were in exactly her predicament, girls who felt as badly as she did over not being chosen. And dozens of other mothers, too, who wished that they'd never heard of sororities.

Mother wrung her hands when everything she said only made Cheryl sob more violently, and at length she curled up beside her and drew the blankets up to her chin. "Let's not talk about it any more tonight, my pet."

Tomorrow is another day, Mother had murmured wearily as she drifted off to sleep. This morning, facing her reflection in the glass, Cheryl was prepared to agree that it was indeed another day, and one on which she could not possibly attend high school.

She couldn't—with eyes so red and lids so puffy that she was peering out through ugly, narrow slits. Mother was on her side; feminine vanity could take only so much and no more. But Father opposed them. Staying away would be cowardly, he insisted. A person had to learn to face up to things. You didn't retreat, you went forward.

"It's going to be tough, Dad." Cheryl's lower lip trembled.

"Whoever said life was easy?" Father looked for confirmation from Mother. No, life hadn't been easy for either of them, and they'd had to earn all they had. They'd married when they were barely out of their teens and had struggled along side by side. Cheryl had been born near a military post when they were living in a poorly furnished room or two which was all that they could afford.

"You have to be brave a lot of times when what you'd rather do is to run." Father reminded her that she was the daughter of a corporal who had seen plenty of action overseas.

World War II might have had its battles; but, as you saw them these days on television, they looked exciting. They were not at all like going to school today at Hunterford High where everyone would know she had failed to make Tri Phi. That called for another kind of courage, and her father was sure that she had it. . . . had what he called by the polite name of "intestinal fortitude."

"Atta, girl," he encouraged her, leaving late for the office and going out of his way to drop her off near the high school. "Show them you're not licked. Get in there and fight."

It might not have been so hard to follow her father's advice if she had not run into Judy and Alicia first thing. They were wearing their pledge ribbons, but the moment they saw her a cloud dimmed their faces. They hadn't known the Tri Phis were leaving her out, they said. They'd kept looking for her to arrive; and, when she didn't, they'd been so upset they hadn't heard half of what was said and hadn't enjoyed the ceremony by which they were pledged.

Then there was Sue Shaw who came up after science class and put her arms around Cheryl. She was terribly sorry. Most of the girls had wanted to pledge her, she told Cheryl. Everything would have gone all right if it hadn't been for . . . Sue hesitated. Cheryl had been blackballed, but Sue wasn't supposed to reveal the name of the person who had done it.

"Was it Ethel Barnes?" Cheryl could feel it in her bones. Ethel had taken this opportunity to get even with her for the time when she had beaten Ethel for class office. That had been in junior high, and they both had run for secretary that first year. Ever since Cheryl was elected, Ethel had carried her grudge.

Cheryl could tell by Sue's face that her guess was correct, and now the whole story came out. Ethel had told them that Cheryl's uncle had been in jail and—well—

was a drunkard. Some of the girls who had been on the fence about Cheryl—as they had been about all the girls who were pledged—began to waver, and then. . . .

"Of course I know that what your uncle does should not make a bit of difference about you. I told them so, but you know how it is. . . ."

Yes, Cheryl did know how it was. It was just as cruel as anything could be. Ethel had dragged out the family skeleton and had used it to defeat her. No matter how Cheryl looked or how she'd dressed or how she'd acted at the rushing tea . . . no matter what a good life her mother and father had built up for themselves . . . no matter that Uncle Elmer had been a wartime hero and had a dozen decorations to show for his bravery!

Sue reached for the box of tissues she kept in her locker as the hot tears flowed down Cheryl's cheeks.

Cheryl had tried to keep her mind off the whole problem in science class; but, as she left Sue to go on to her next period, she was not sure she could continue through the day. Girls resplendent with pledge ribbons from the various sororities walked four and five abreast, all but flying banners of triumph. So many students crowded around to congratulate them that Cheryl could scarcely make her way through the hubbub to her social problems class.

She had a social problem of her own today. As she entered the classroom, she felt that everyone was looking at her with the knowledge that she had failed. When you tried for a sorority and did not make the grade, you were sure that everyone must consider you an absolute dud. Cheryl was so busy with her own thoughts that she did not notice other woebegone faces in the room, nor did she at first hear the sound of weeping.

A girl toward the back of the room had lost all control and was sobbing face down on her desk. It was the signal for the dam to break among all of the discards. Two girls were in such an emotional state that they burst into hysterics. Only Cheryl wept silently.

"Broken hearts all over the place," the teacher said, not unsympathetically, putting in a hurried call for the school nurse or one of her staff. The boy he had sent came back to report, in effect, that pandemonium reigned all through the school. The wave of hysteria had spread from sophomores even to upperclassmen, and the school was in an uproar.

The Dean of Women was calling mothers to come get daughters who had broken down under stress—to take them home and quiet them. Something ought to be done about sororities, everyone was saying; they had no right to cause such an uproar.

Soon, a delegation of mothers was holding an indignation meeting on the front steps of the high school, saying that sororities ought to be banned. Mothers were saying they would write to the mayor and take the matter up with the school board.

"If it wasn't sororities, it would be something else." Mrs. Kramer tried to interject a note of sense as she stood with Cheryl.

"Yes," agreed another woman who expressed herself in scholarly fashion. "It's the herd instinct that's particularly strong during this adolescent age. A wanting to conform, to belong. That's what makes it so hard to be left out."

"You can say that again," a red-faced woman declared, vowing she'd never let another daughter of hers go through that particular wringer. They'd spent so much money on the girl's outfit, and she'd always been so popular.

"I'm afraid we've given our girls a false sense of values," the studious-looking woman murmured, her voice lost in the general outcry. "It's probably our fault as much as it's theirs."

As Cheryl followed her mother away from the throng of outraged parents and weeping offspring, she breathed a deep sigh. She was proud of Mother for not getting involved in the frenzy of the crowd. After the tension of the past few days, she felt suddenly weak.

"Let's get away from these crazy people," Mother said, stepping on the accelerator to suit her action to the word. "I never saw such a mess."

Father would understand when she and Mother explained to him, Cheryl thought. It would be foolish to try to stay here in school to fight when all the others were leaving the premises. She curled up in the backseat of the car while Mother shopped for the groceries and ran other errands that kept them out for the rest of the morning.

Mother made few attempts at conversation, and Cheryl was grateful to be left alone. Little was expected of her besides deciding where she'd prefer to have lunch

—the Mexican place that served tacos or one of the Chinese restaurants. Mother was making a valiant effort to make this seem like a holiday, but both of them knew that they had precious little to celebrate.

Because Mother had no appointments today for fittings or modeling, she could devote the day to her daughter. Now she suggested that they go to call on Cousin Dorothy. Though it had not been said in so many words, both of them seemed reluctant to go back to the house. A visit would postpone it. There was no use now to conceal Cheryl's fiasco from Dorothy or from anyone else.

Dorothy would want to know why she was out of school today—Dorothy would ask a thousand questions. Mother would have to be the one to answer, for Cheryl was not in a mood to talk. She was only going along for the ride.

They found Dorothy out on the lawn taking a sunbath in an old faded playsuit that made her look about Cheryl's age. As she leaped up to welcome them, Cheryl was no longer in awe of her. She seemed less of the campus queen today, and more like a person who might share your troubles.

As she listened to Mother's account, Dorothy plucked at the grass, throwing up little tufts of it with an air of growing disturbance. It brought back her own high school days and her own time of heartbreak, she said. Hadn't her own mother ever told them about it? She hadn't made a high school sorority either, and it had been a terrible blow.

"Seems like the end of the world, doesn't it?" She put an arm around Cheryl. "I can laugh about it now, but I haven't forgotten."

She hadn't made a college sorority right at first either, she went on to admit, but she had plunged into all kinds of activities and now was on the dean's honor list for scholarship, too, as well as belonging to a sorority. "Sometimes I think it makes you a better and stronger person not to have everything fall into your lap."

Mother nodded in agreement while Cheryl listened dully, not prepared to apply anything they said to herself. No matter what Dorothy said, she could not imagine anyone laughing, ever, about a hurt that went so deep.

Dorothy was different. Dorothy was a big success. With her big brown eyes and heart-shaped face, she was far more attractive than Cheryl could possibly expect to be at twenty or at any age. Dorothy was so pretty and so clever that she'd always be ahead of Cheryl Kramer.

But she was glad when Dorothy accepted Mother's invitation to come along home with them for dinner and part of the evening. A tight family threesome could become oppressive tonight. With Dorothy as a guest, Father wouldn't be so apt to start one of his lectures, and Mother would have a distraction. When you were having your troubles, being an only child could be a real drawback. You could be smothered with love and attention.

What Cheryl wanted most was a few hours to herself when she'd not have to react and not have to talk. She left Mother to entertain Dorothy and shut the door of her room. Muffling the phone with a pillow and drawing the blinds against the bright afternoon sun, she threw herself down on the bed. The outside world could wait for her.

11 *Field Expedition*

It must have been well after dinnertime when Cheryl awakened, for night had fallen outside. As she listened for familiar sounds, she heard her mother greeting Judy and Alicia. Someone must have driven them over to see her, Cheryl thought. Their voices were high and shrill. They were sorry Cheryl wasn't to be disturbed because they needed to talk to her.

Forgetting her tear-stained face and her earlier qualms about not wanting to see anyone, Cheryl hurried down the hall. Judy and Alicia were special, and

135

she'd talk to them any day in the week.

There had been such commotion after she and the others had left, they reported, that classes never really got down to business. As for themselves, they hadn't been able to think about anything except Cheryl and the pact they had made only yesterday. What a long time ago that seemed! The three of them had vowed to stick together, and Judy and Alicia weren't about to go back on their word. A promise was a promise.

They'd talked it over with their families, too, and Alicia's father had driven them over because he was proud of them for wanting to do what was right. Cheryl could hear him now, out in the garage where Father had his workshop. He was leaving this discussion up to the female contingent.

"You see it's like this," Alicia explained. "We hate to see you feel so bad—"

"And we'll turn in our pledge ribbons if you want us to," Judy finished in a rush of enthusiasm. "Show those old Tri Phis we don't care a hoot what they think of us."

"You'd do that for Cheryl?" Mother interposed, her voice unbelieving.

"Yes, or tell them that we won't belong unless they take Cheryl, too." Judy and Alicia said it together. "We're friends, aren't we?"

"Yes." Mother's eyes grew moist as she hurried out of the room, lest she influence the decision. Youthful idealism and the sacrifice they were offering were almost too much for her.

"Gee, I'll have to think about it." Cheryl, too, was all

but overcome by this demonstration of loyalty. She slumped to the sofa. It was such an awful lot to ask of anyone, to give up what had figured recently in all of their dreams—the parties and the fun that were part of belonging to the "upper crust" in high school. If she were the one who had been pledged, would she offer to step back because of Judy and Alicia? It was a hard question to answer, and this was a hard decision to make.

She could see Judy and Alicia slipping away from her into Tri Phi activities, leaving her behind among the forgotten. As she considered this, she felt increasingly sorry for herself.

Yet there was no hiding the fact that the Tri Phis did not want her. They had made that as plain as the nose on your face. Nothing Judy and Alicia could do would soften this blow to her pride. The Tri Phis did not consider her good enough for them. That was the whole truth, and everyone in high school who mattered knew it. Cheryl Kramer did not rate.

She shook her head because she did not trust herself to speak as the tears filled her eyes. Judy and Alicia stopped their nervous thumbing of magazines and came over to sit beside her, one on either side. Tri Phi would not come between them, they insisted; they wouldn't let it. The warm current of their feeling flowed; they'd be friends forever and ever.

"Well, it was a good try, but it didn't work." Alicia came down to earth as her father returned to collect his two passengers and gave her a questioning look.

"Yes, it was." Mrs. Kramer, in the next room, had

overheard the conversation. Now she embraced Judy and Alicia. "And I want you to know we appreciate it. More than I can say, or Cheryl can."

When Cheryl went back to high school on the following day, nothing seemed real to her. As other discards came up to mourn with her, she heard them only through her own fog of despair.

One set of parents, more frantic than Cheryl's had been, were taking their daughter up to San Francisco this weekend to help her forget. Another girl had been promised a car for her birthday. A third, whose family couldn't afford it, was to get a new party dress and slippers and go to a dance. Another was having a pajama party on Saturday night and wanted Cheryl to come.

Most parents were doing their best to make up for the disappointment, but all Cheryl's father had to suggest was one of his basketball games. She hated to tag along like a little girl when her father refereed for the sports clubs. There could be good-looking players on some of the teams, but Father always spoiled it for her by telling them her age. Instead of flirting with her, they brought her popcorn. Well, really! She'd rather stay home.

That was what she proceeded to do. Mother was going out to her bridge club and suggested driving Cheryl and Feeney Chase to the movies, but Cheryl refused. She'd not yet come to that—to having Feeney Chase as a constant companion. She was not about to have Feeney Chase draped around her neck for the rest of her days.

When a girl's life had been shattered to bits, all she felt up to doing was just sitting among the ruins. The pajama party the next night was a flop. Cheryl had known it would be. You couldn't get a group of mourners together and expect to have any fun. It was more like a wake.

Nobody wanted to dance or play Ping-pong or cards. Feeble attempts at joking fell as flat as so many pizzas. Besides, she didn't know many of the girls very well. The crowd had only one thing in common: They were a bunch of misfits, and they were painfully aware of it.

"Misery loves company, and I'm misery," one of the girls said, expressing the general spirit of the evening.

These days, a pall lay over everything for Cheryl. A black mist settled down over the minutes and the hours and made them twice as long. Could it have been only a week since she had heard the bad news? It seemed like a year to her. She was picking at her food and losing weight, the only bright spot in this whole dismal time. The first of her three wishes was being granted, at any rate, though the second one was as remote as ever and she had been refused the third one.

Noting how pale and listless she was, Grandmother suggested sulphur and molasses. It was an old-fashioned remedy that she always gave her children in the spring, and it was especially beneficial for growing girls, she said. Ugh! Cheryl shuddered at the thought of how the concoction must taste. The very name of it sounded perfectly horrible.

And she wasn't a growing girl any longer; that wasn't her trouble. She hadn't added an inch in a year, and it was high time she stopped. Almost five feet seven was

tall enough for any girl to reach, and already she tow-
ered over most of the boys she knew, or admired. Maybe
they hadn't stopped growing yet—she could always
hope. Currently, however, it was one of her problems.

Bill Meyers was plenty tall enough for her; she had
no worries on that score, but plenty of them on others.
She'd never get acquainted with him now that she wasn't
going to be a sorority girl. It had been her observation
that fraternity men seldom dated girls who didn't belong to sororities, and her faint chance of meeting him
in any other way had disappeared. He wasn't working in
the library, and she had seen him recently only on-stage
in the school auditorium.

All her hopes were vanishing. She was going nowhere
so fast that even Father was alarmed. She had never
stayed so long in her own private Slough of Despond,
and he and Mother were beginning to wonder whether
changing high schools might help. Or sending her to a
private school which they could ill afford.

It was unnatural for a girl her age to spend as much
time in her room, sitting on the bed and staring into
space or wandering aimlessly about the house until she
was getting on the nerves of both parents. The worst of
it was that they felt themselves to be partly to blame.

Grandmother, always the voice of conscience, pointed
this out to them one evening when she didn't think
Cheryl was listening. They'd overprotected her and in-
dulged her until she had come to think that the world
was her oyster. They hadn't prepared her to meet up
with failure. "That's the trouble with all the young

folks these days." Grandmother was severe. "You've put them in cotton batting until they don't know how to fend for themselves."

So she was soft and weak! Grandmother had said so, not realizing how her voice could carry to the other parts of the house. Cheryl was in the laundry room ironing blouses, but she could hear every word being spoken. Changing schools wouldn't help because Cheryl would take herself with her wherever she went, and so forth and so on. What she had to do was change her attitude instead. "She'll be a better person for it." Grandmother was using almost the same words as Cousin Dorothy. Perhaps, after all, both of them might know what they were talking about.

It was clear to Cheryl that she had to do something, no matter what. Crying herself to sleep every night did not improve her appearance. She might be almost thin, but she could hardly call herself interesting-looking. With her skirts sagging in the back because the waistbands needed tightening, and her sweaters drooping from her shoulders, she was no beauty prize. The long and short of it was that she was sick and tired of being sick and tired.

You took yourself with you wherever you went, Grandmother had said, and she'd be great company for herself on the field expedition. All year the science class had been looking forward to this annual outing. As the appointed Saturday grew near, enthusiasm mounted. They were going to explore a landslide that had revealed a wealth of fossil formations. Students from other high

schools were to join them at The Palisades—students
from Hollywood and even from the San Fernando Valley.

The girls were hoping to meet fascinating new boys.
They quickly decided that ordinary hiking clothes—old
jeans and jackets—would not be sufficiently glamorous.
Most of them were going in pastel capris, and they were
searching out sunglasses in the most exotic shapes and
colors that the Economy Drug Store could supply.

The way Cheryl still felt about life in general, she
would only be going along for the ride; but, as they all
clambered into the chartered bus that was to take them
to their destination, her spirits began to rise. She was
glad she was wearing her green denim outfit trimmed in
white fringe for a casual air; other girls were admiring
it along with the beach bag shaped like a whale in which
she carried her lunch. With all the climbing around the
rocks which they expected to do, the outfit was likely
to be ruined before the day was half over, but Mother
had told her not to worry about it. They had bought it
on clearance at the end of last season and, besides, everything that composed it would wash. Mother was so
happy that, for a change, Cheryl was taking an interest
in going anywhere that she gave her a bright scarf that
was perfect with the denim outfit.

As they traveled near the ocean, some of the boys
groaned when they saw the height and the force of the
waves. It was a perfect day for riding in on the surf, and
the highway was lined with the cars of more fortunate
youths who had arrived with their surfboards and were

busy unloading them. What a waste to spend such a day on a crazy old fossil hunt!

"That's not what we came to hunt for," one of the girls giggled, setting off a flurry of good-natured banter.

Then somebody struck up "Barnacle Bill" on a harmonica, and they all joined in the chorus, making up new words as they went. "Keep it clean, kids," the science teacher ordered when some of the improvisations threatened to get out of line.

The bus was so noisy a girl couldn't hear herself think, much less start to brood. For the first time in days, Cheryl was able to forget about her troubles and to wrap them up "in the old kit-bag," as the next song suggested.

Singing and fooling as they went, they continued on up the shore. Some of the boys moved back to sit with certain girls, but most remained up in the front which suited Cheryl perfectly. She felt too shy to maintain animated conversation with the opposite sex, outside of the classroom. She was even more unsure of her attractions than ever since her failure with Tri Phi. She was content to sit and enjoy the general hubbub without taking a major role.

When they reached The Palisades, she stayed close to the small group around the science teacher. Other girls clambered out of the bus and quickly scattered to make a "general survey of the field," which meant boys from other high schools. Cheryl remained with the serious students, however, the ones actually interested in fossil discoveries.

The giant landslide had exposed a wealth of fossil treasures if you had the eyes to discover it. There was petrified wood from the ancient shores of the sea . . . the delicate imprints of plants . . . the shells of marine creatures imprisoned through ages. You could see how a starfish had looked a thousand years ago, and observe the outlines of fish no longer in existence but which, the teacher said, had given rise to present species in the long course of evolution.

On the cliffs far above them, handsome houses teetered on the brink of the destruction that was revealing these pages from eons past—a gash in the cliffs caused by winter rains. Tons of earth had been loosened and had gone hurtling down across the coastal highway and on into the sea. People living up there must wonder when they, too, might be turned into fossils, Cheryl thought, as the teacher told of several unfortunate folk who had been caught when the land gave way.

He warned them to stay close to the bottom of the rubble lest more landslides start, and she was surprised when she saw a tiny figure making its way down the cliffs from a perilous height. It must be someone who was fearless or foolhardy, someone who was ignoring all these signs that, in large red letters, spelled DANGER.

As the figure loomed larger, she sensed something familiar about it. She could not quite place what it was, but she knew she had seen this person elsewhere. Whoever it was was leaping from rock to rock and, occasionally, sliding down a precipice. She almost hated to watch. Others also had observed this daredevil descent, so that a gallery of spectators gathered.

"Darn fool kid," the various teachers were saying, each trying to check the members of his or her classes to be sure that none of them were so flagrantly disobeying strict orders.

When finally the boy jumped down to safer territory near them, he swept off the tattered straw hat which he wore and bowed low. "Great performance, wasn't it?" he said. "Sorry I couldn't oblige you by putting on a real show—like maybe getting killed."

He strode insolently away to join one of the groups where a scolding awaited him. "Fine thing if a chap can't drop down out of his own backyard when he's a mind to," he answered indignantly, pointing to one of the houses endangered by the slide.

Cheryl hovered on the outskirts, wanting to be sure of his identity before she spoke to him. The boy had reminded her of Peter Guinness. Now she had no doubt of it. Whoever would have guessed that Peter was a high school student or that he lived in what was practically a mansion?

"Still watching whales, I see," he said, wiping his face with a grimy sleeve and pointing to her beach bag.

He had recognized her immediately. She must have made more of an impression on him than she had originally thought. The fishing boat took out hundreds of passengers in the course of a day, but she hadn't remained a mere blur.

"Anything to eat in that silly old bag?" However rudely he expressed it, he was choosing her as a luncheon partner. She realized this when he asked her what she wanted to drink and then he strode to a stand near the road to take his place in line with dozens of other boys.

"Wherever did you meet him? They say his father is a big movie director." Several girls from Cheryl's class gathered about her, obviously hoping for an introduction when Peter returned.

"Oh, I get around." Cheryl tossed her head with what she hoped was a careless gesture. She'd never admit now that it had been on a fishing boat and that she had disliked him intensely. Peter might be worth second-knowing.

She was glad now that she had brought extra sandwiches and deviled eggs and cake. Though Peter came back with hot dogs for each of them, he had an apparently bottomless stomach. "Got to keep up my strength, you know," he said, going around to collect further food from other girls who were eager to attract his attention.

"Now, you take whale bones, kiddo. . . ." Peter returned with what looked to be rocks and tossed them into Cheryl's lap. They were of a reddish color and had a porosity at either end, through which the life-giving fluids had flowed. "You can always tell a petrified whale bone," Peter said. "It's obvious."

"Are you always thinking about whales?" Cheryl wanted to shift the conversation around to himself.

"Oh, no. Lots of things up here." He tapped at his head. He had a fresh crew cut, so short that he was almost bald. No wonder she'd had difficulty at first in recognizing him! The bristling shock of black hair was gone, but the eyes were the same, restless and searching and of a tawny shade that resembled a cat's.

"That fishing boat job was for Saturdays, but I got tired of it." He yawned and stretched. "I get tired of things pretty quick, and right now I'm sick of this bunch of goofs. Sophomoric minds . . . they shouldn't have been let out of grade school."

Was she being included in his general disdain for his high school contemporaries? Cheryl was inclined to think so as he lay back against a rock and stared up at the sky. With no brothers to instruct her, she was not too familiar with boys and their habits. Maybe it was not unusual for them to ignore you and seem to forget that you were sitting nearby.

She was saying that she'd have to be going when he leaped to his feet. "Why not come up to my house and we'll have a swim?"

"But—but—" Cheryl looked at the cliff doubtfully. She had no wish to climb all those perilous hundreds of feet.

"There's a road, silly. And my mother's at home. You'll be perfectly chaperoned." He mimicked a prissy schoolteacher's voice.

"Suppose we don't get back before the bus leaves? I haven't any other way to—" What would Mother say and what would her teacher say if she didn't return with the crowd?

12 *Surprise Meeting*

Thanks to Peter, Cheryl had plenty of specimens to show to her science teacher as an excuse for leaving a group that was still engaged in fossil hunts and flirtations. Peter would get her back on time, she said, making a point of it so that Peter would overhear. She wasn't about to be left in the lurch somewhere along the Pacific Coast Highway.

"Comme çi, comme ça." Peter shrugged his shoulders.

"Freely translated, that's French for 'maybe,' and I can't have that, young man. She's either here, or

else. . . ." With the responsibility of so many young people on his hands, the teacher looked understandably
worried.

"Or else I'll drive her back to Belmont Beach myself.
Here's a fellow who can vouch for me." Peter indicated
his own teacher who had come up beside them.

Cheryl heard the man mumble something about "ec-
centric but responsible" and "near-genius I.Q." before
Peter impatiently dragged her away with him. Clearly,
he was not nearly as wild as he appeared at times,
Cheryl thought, making excuses for doing what she
wanted to do which was to see Peter's house. If his
father was a movie director, it must be sensational. And,
if they were going to be late, she'd call her mother collect and reassure her. A person didn't often get a chance
like this to rub shoulders with the upper echelons of
Hollywood. She'd have a lot to tell Judy and Alicia
when she saw them on Monday.

"What a pretty girl! So natural-looking, too." The
freckle-faced woman grubbing about the plants that
landscaped the front of the Guinness grounds looked up
and begged pardon for not shaking hands.

"That's Mother, in case you didn't know," Peter said,
not bothering with introductions.

"I'm Cheryl Kramer." She remembered suddenly that
Peter did not even know her name and hadn't asked. He
seemed to think that "kiddo" sufficed.

"Follow me if you can stand it." Peter plunged on between the stone urns that stood on either side of the
imposing front door and led the way into a salon that

was heavily draped in damask. Weaving a course around gilded coffee tables and deeply luxurious chairs grouped around a massive carved fireplace, he said, "This is our Hollywood set, and I wouldn't be caught dead in it." He did a leapfrog over a tapestry-covered footstool and arrived in the kitchen whence delicious smells issued.

"Mamie's been cooking brownies for me," he said, scooping up a handful of the cookies from a tray and expecting Cheryl to follow suit. "We'll come back for the rest."

He pushed open the door that led to the pool and disappeared into a striped canvas cabaña. Emerging in bathing trunks presently, he ran out to the end of the diving board.

"Do you follow me?" he asked, apparently slightly puzzled to see Cheryl still standing there.

"I don't have anything to wear." The boy must be an idiot, Cheryl thought. Nobody plunged into a pool in green denims.

"I see . . . the slight matter of a bathing suit. Take your choice among the ladies." He gestured to another of the cabañas which, as Cheryl explored it, revealed everything from bikinis to bloomered suits from some old-fashioned comedy. She was not about to go in for laughs; so she chose, instead, a stunning sheath in gold lamé.

"Green would be better. Your eyes are rather nice, you know. Not a bad figure either." For once, Peter had stopped his antics long enough to take a good look at her. "H-m-m, not bad. A bit lumpy, but. . . ."

She hoped he wasn't going to spoil the afternoon by an attempt to start cuddling; but this, apparently, was farthest from his mind. He expected her to dive through the colored hoops that floated upon the surface of the pool and make a game of it. If you could hit center from the diving board, it counted five. From the side of the pool, the count was three.

"Shall we keep her, Mom?" he asked, as Mrs. Guinness came through the gate to watch the competition.

"At least until after dinner." Mrs. Guinness had a nice smile that made her eyes crinkle up at the corners.

"Good heavens, is it that late?" Cheryl hadn't noticed the lowering rays of the sun. "I'll have to call my mother."

"Tell her you'll arrive special delivery." Peter had crawled to a rubber swan in the middle of the pool and was resting.

"If there's any trouble, I'll talk to her," Mrs. Guinness offered, indicating a telephone obscured by the tree ferns that surrounded the pool. "We don't go inside when we're dripping."

"Of course." Cheryl shuddered at the thought of what pool water might do to the elegant salon through which they had passed.

"We try to keep our meals simple when the cook's away," Mrs. Guinness said, drawing out a barbecue stand on wheels and telling Peter to start the charcoal fire. "When his father's here, he likes to have it exactly right for the steaks, but," her tone was wistful, "Mr. Guinness is on location in Italy."

"So I'm the head of the house." Peter stood tall behind his mother as Cheryl looked beyond them to the ferns and the waterfall that poured into the pool to make it a green oasis of enchantment. Yes, a big house like this must often get lonely with only two people to fill it.

"Tell me more about yourself, dear." Since Mrs. Guinness seemed truly interested, Cheryl poured out her story. She told more than she had intended—even about the heartache of the past few weeks. Peter, too, listened sympathetically.

"I didn't know girls felt like that," he said. "It's all a bunch of rot, and you've got to learn to ignore it."

He rolled potatoes in foil and thrust them into the blaze, then cut up the salad greens. "He takes over when our cook leaves for the weekend." Mrs. Guinness poured vinegar and oil for the dressing and added big chunks of roquefort cheese. "Say when."

"You can't add too much to suit me." Cheryl loved roquefort.

"It's better in the desert." Peter scowled as his mother brought out a rich silver service and a pastel linen cloth to set on one of the round tables. The table had a huge sun umbrella above it which Peter proceeded to close; now that the air was growing chill, protection from the sun was the last thing one needed. Cheryl shivered in her bathing suit and went into the cabaña to dress, but Peter capered about in his trunks until his mother made him put on a sweat shirt.

"You make me cold just to look at you," she said,

warming her hands over the charcoal fire. They were beautiful hands sparkling with rings set with rubies and emeralds that were probably real. The wife of an important movie director wouldn't be apt to wear costume jewelry. Mother would want to hear about them and about what she wore for intimate little dinners—white sharkskin slacks and a blue jersey top with gold slippers.

"You can see the stars better in the desert," Peter said, squinting up at the sky before he bit into his steak.

"Peter loves the desert," his mother explained. "We don't fuss a bit down there. And you must come to see us."

"Why not? Too much civilization around here." Peter scorned the linen napkins and went in to find the paper ones that were more to his liking.

"Peter's a natural-born savage," Mrs. Guinness sighed, "but I suppose all boys are, more or less."

"They are in my high school, but I don't know too many. Very well, that is," Cheryl admitted.

"Don't worry, there's plenty of time for it, my dear. And I find your honesty refreshing. I haven't met many girls quite like you."

"Guess I'm one-of-a-kind. That's what Dad always says." Cheryl was happy to be so much at ease with Mrs. Guinness. She remembered Mrs. Moore and the rushing tea. Older women seemed to like her. If only she got on half as well with her own generation!

Peter seemed already bored with her, but it was hard to tell about Peter. He was wandering around restlessly inside the house and out again until he suggested that he show her his various collections.

"Not tonight, dear," Mrs. Guinness interposed. "Cheryl has to get home sometime, you know, and once you get started on all those relics of yours. . . ."

Cheryl was surprised when Mrs. Guinness prepared to accompany them on what would be a long drive. It would be cold in the open car, she said, bringing out cashmere sweaters for her and for Cheryl. Peter could sulk all he liked, she remarked, but that wouldn't change her arrangements. He did not yet have his full driver's license, and she was taking no risk of his being picked up on the freeways.

As the long, slim, white foreign car rolled out of the garage with Mrs. Guinness at the wheel and Peter opened the door for his guest, Cheryl chuckled at his rebellious expression. He was not allowed to make the difficult turn into the street, it seemed, but, with his mother aboard, he could drive the rest of the way. Peter —fish boy and cliff climber—was under parental wraps.

Cheryl settled down between Peter and his mother, grateful for the weight of her authority. Left to himself, Peter was the type to drive ninety miles an hour with squad cars following, and Cheryl would have been terrified. As they neared Canterbury Knolls, she grew silent. Peter was still barefooted and in his sweat shirt and trunks. She was concerned about the impression he'd make on her family and afraid that her father would never let her hear the last of it. Peter looked like a "beach-bum," and Father highly disapproved of the breed he resembled.

But Peter settled the problem for her in his usual high-handed fashion. He was not about to come in and meet anyone, he said, and that was that.

"I do hope your mother won't think we are frightfully rude, but. . . ." Mrs. Guinness gestured helplessly as though there were certain things even she could not force Peter to do. "Another time, dear. You're good for Peter, I think."

With the approach of spring vacation, Cheryl was again down in the dumps. Here she expected to stay. All the sororities were renting cottages down at Balboa Island and other places along the shore for the Easter week house parties that were a long-established tradition among the young people all over southern California. Cheryl had longed to join these Easter week festivities when she was old enough to do so. This year it was not her age which excluded her—Judy and Alicia were going with the Tri Phis. It was useless for Mother to offer, by way of consolation, to drive Cheryl and some of her non-sorority friends to spend one of the days at Disneyland.

There'd have been a battle with Father about a sorority house party, of course, but she was sure she'd have won it. Somehow she would have gotten around Father's dislike of this whole "Easter-bunny" business. The newspapers were full of plans to control the young vacationers, and, as in other years, the headlines were screaming. Between the newspapers and her father, one would think that every high school or college student who went to one of these house parties was headed for trouble. "Easter-bunny" was a bad word around the Kramer household and elsewhere.

Father would never need to worry about her, Cheryl thought. His daughter was too unpopular to be anything but a "goody-good" without the slightest chance of getting into mischief.

Peter hadn't called her, but that was no great disappointment. Peter wasn't the sort of boy who was apt, ever, to be a regular date. Besides, he might have tumbled down the cliff by now along with his house, though Mrs. Guinness had said they were in no immediate danger.

While Cheryl had made much of Peter when she talked to Judy and Alicia and they had been impressed, she had, within these several weeks, practically exhausted the subject.

Now, again, life seemed a wasteland. On the first morning of spring vacation, she wandered about the house in an old pair of shorts and a faded blouse that was as tattered as her spirits. When the mailman came up the walk and said he had a letter for her, she took it listlessly. Nobody interesting ever wrote her a letter, and she was surprised to see that it was postmarked Palm Springs. Inside, in thin spidery writing that she could hardly decipher, was a note signed "Pauline Guinness."

Mother was more adept at reading difficult handwriting than she was. Now, as Cheryl hastened to find her, she wondered whether her first impression of the note had been correct. Was it a for-real invitation from Mrs. Guinness, or was it not?

"Well, I don't see any reason why you can't go, but we'll have to check with your father. You said she seemed to be a very nice person." Getting down to particulars, Mother read the invitation more slowly.

Mrs. Guinness was suggesting that Cheryl spend several days with her and Peter down in their desert hideaway. Cheryl could take the bus to Palm Springs where they'd meet her, and she was to bring only her very oldest clothes and hiking shoes. She was sorry to be so late with her invitation, and she hoped Cheryl could make it. If so, call collect and so forth and so on.

"Doesn't sound very fancy, does it? Not much like Palm Springs." Cheryl had been thrilled at the idea of visiting this alluring resort, but now she was less enthusiastic. "I guess I'm not a very fancy person."

But Mother seemed pleased that Cheryl had the prospect of a spring outing and encouraged her to accept. Even if she couldn't join the merry crowd down at the shore, as she had hoped to do this year, she could find her fun elsewhere. And Father agreed.

He could drive her into Los Angeles when he went to his office and drop her off at the bus station. Leaving her parents to make plans for the journey, Cheryl went into her room to decide what to pack in her bag.

She wasn't leaving until the latter part of the week, but it was something to look forward to anyway, especially since Father told her that the bus station was in a sordid section of town. Her interest was aroused when he warned her that, under no circumstances, was she to walk out of the building. It was no place for a nice girl to be, in the broad light of day or any other time, he repeated the morning of her departure. Mother repeated her last-minute instructions several times and took so long about them that Father grew impatient.

"I'm only going away for a few days, Mom," Cheryl protested. Mother was making such a fuss over her that one would think she were leaving for Europe.

Now, as they whizzed along the freeway in the heavy morning traffic, Father wondered aloud whether he ought to come into the bus station with her and buy the ticket. Like Mother, he was—Cheryl searched for the phrase her grandmother used—overprotecting her. Was she never going to be allowed to take any responsibility for herself?

"Good gracious, Dad, they don't kidnap people out of bus stations, do they?"

"You have a point," her father admitted. "If you think you can manage. . . ."

"Why shouldn't I? Other girls travel on buses, don't they? And right out of Los Angeles, too." It was the first journey Cheryl had ever undertaken on her own. While it was no great distance, she was beginning to enjoy the feeling of independence which it gave her.

Besides, as Father recounted the various dangers that might await her, she grew more and more fascinated. She was not to talk to any servicemen . . . she was to hold tight to her purse . . . she'd best keep a close watch on her traveling bag. Whoever would have thought that a fairly short trip on an overland bus could hold so many possibilities for mishap?

She chuckled as she stood in line later at the ticket window, surrounded by mothers with babies and stair-steps of tots, and by vaguely middle-aged folk. Even Father could not have discovered a sinister face in the whole lot of them. It was going to be a dull and highly respectable trip, she thought, wandering over to buy a magazine and wishing she hadn't promised Father not to go outside and explore.

She could have checked her bag in one of the lockers and seen a good bit of this part of Los Angeles before her bus was scheduled to leave. The little she had glimpsed of the streets as Father drove her along them had intrigued her. They were colorful with burlesque houses and gospel missions and street peddlers. The crowds that milled through them, even at this hour of the day, were alien to a girl who led a sheltered life. One could only wonder what stories lay behind these beaten faces of men and of women, and what dramas might take place up the shabby steps of these cheap hotels with their dingy curtains and their tattered window shades.

She stood at the glass front of the bus station and, sipping an orange drink, looked out for as long as she dared without missing her bus altogether.

13 *Desert Hideaway*

Cheryl found a place next to one of the windows of the large transcontinental bus and wished she were heading with it to El Paso, Texas. She had never been out of the state of California, and it was more than high time.

The woman who had squeezed into the seat beside her was going on to Chicago, she said, placing her purse on her ample lap and promptly producing pictures of grandchildren. "One here looks just like you," she said, pointing to a face that was fuzzily out of focus in a large family group. The woman was a regular talking-machine, Cheryl thought disgustedly.

Several girls around Cheryl's age had been last to board the bus. Now, as they chatted with several young sailors, Cheryl wished she could join them, instead of being stuck with a grandmother who was rapidly boring her to death. The sailors looked as merry and as innocent as some of the boys in her classes at high school. Father couldn't possibly have meant that any harm could result from being friendly.

Apparently, the girls were headed for Palm Springs also. As the gay scraps of conversation drifted toward her, Cheryl grew more and more restive. They were talking about all the fun they expected to have in Palm Springs during the rest of Easter week, and here she was headed for some isolated spot in the desert far away from the bright lights and the general excitement. Girls like these had so much more freedom than her own parents ever allowed her. The way things were going she'd never be allowed to grow up. A girl of fifteen was no longer a baby who had to be watched every minute. She should be expected to have a little bit of sense.

Palm Springs had loads of attractive shops and cute clothes to buy, the girls said, but she would never have so much as a look at them. Peter left her in no doubt of this when he met her at the resort bus station in an old beat-up jeep that looked as though it had been through the Second World War. "Let's get out of here fast," he said, meaning the whole of Palm Springs and, in particular, the crowds that were roaming the streets. They were of high school and college age, and Peter declared they must all have an inferiority complex. It was immature, he said, to need a group to make you feel important.

"And what are we?" Cheryl held to the sides of the jeep which was bouncing her about like a pebble in a box. Peter might want to be different, but she'd prefer to be part of the "common herd." She'd picked up this phrase from Peter, along with others like "inferiority complex," but she did not share his attitude.

He left the road and started on a straight line across the desert wastes which surrounded the city. When they came to low dunes, he climbed over them; nothing stopped Peter or the progress of his jeep. He might shout over the roar of the motor that this was the only way to see the desert, but Cheryl was beginning to doubt that she'd ever survive it. The jeep had no springs to speak of, just as Peter had no fear. He was trying some of the steeper hills, also, and, when they couldn't make the run to the top in one dash, he went back down to make another attempt.

All Cheryl could do was to hold on for dear life, though what she would have preferred was to pick up her bag and run. But, even if Peter had stopped long enough for her to leave this jouncing vehicle, she would not have known what direction to take. One part of the desert looked like the next, and there was not a shade tree to be seen against the jagged horizon.

They were far from civilization and from anything familiar to her when Peter veered abruptly toward what looked from this distance like a gray pile of rocks that

had been tossed at the foot of the mountains. Blue-violet
and soft rose in the changing light, the mountains
dominated the desert with a harsh and hostile beauty.

Nothing in this wild country was friendly to human
beings, Cheryl thought, not the cacti with their bristling spines nor the scanty shrubs that offered no protection whatever from the merciless beat of the sun. She
shuddered as they sped past whitened bones that were
an all-too-vivid reminder of pioneer tales—stories of
wagon trains that had foundered in the desert and the
men, women, and children who had perished from
thirst.

Her head was throbbing from the heat and the glare,
and her throat was parched. Altogether, she was taking
an extremely dim view of this crazy, crazy adventure. As
the wind blew sand against her face in stinging particles,
she thought longingly of Canterbury Knolls and her
own cool green lawn with the sprinklers playing upon
it. She should never have accepted Mrs. Guinness's invitation and consented to accompany Peter to the edge
of nowhere and beyond.

With her head down as a partial shield from the wind
which had sprung up, she did not at first see the outlines
of a house emerging from what had previously looked
like a rock pile. Great boulders were scattered about it
where nature had left them, and the massive walls themselves were of rocks so that the structure blended with
the mountains that all but enclosed it. No wonder Mrs.
Guinness had called it a hideaway! A person would be
unlikely to find it unless he knew the exact location.

"Well, here we are," Peter said unnecessarily, leaping out of the jeep with Cheryl's bag in his grasp. He did not offer to help her descend from her perch, but raced toward the house with a whoop and halloo.

They could have taken a regular road, Cheryl thought crossly, noticing that cars were passing along a not-too-distant highway. Peter needn't have taken her on this careening plunge across the desert and jolted her practically out of her senses. As she sat there, shaken and windburned and preparing not to like any part of her visit, Mrs. Guinness appeared to welcome her.

Peter had disappeared somewhere in the colorful interior of the house; and, for all Cheryl cared, he could stay out of her sight. She settled comfortably in a deep chair covered with black-and-white horsehide and admired the Navajo rugs that enlivened the floor. A huge fireplace at one end of the room was hung with burnished kettles and Indian pots. Altogether, the place had a rugged charm that she could enjoy if Peter left her alone.

When he returned presently with glasses and a pitcher of ice water, she was not prepared to forgive him. Her head ached and she was not in the mood for further entertainment of the sort she'd just experienced. Let the little boy go out and play with his jeep all he liked while she took the nap that Mrs. Guinness thoughtfully suggested.

She was led into a room with a red tile floor and more of the Navajo rugs and Indian baskets that were the keynote of this house which so well expressed the spirit of the desert. Cheryl was beginning to sense more of this as she looked out of the window and caught a pastel and dreamlike view.

"Isn't the palo verde lovely when it's in blossom?" Mrs. Guinness came over to stand beside her and admire the showers of gold over chartreuse-green branches. Several small and frail-appearing trees stood in radiant outline against the purple shadows of the mountains. "It's different every hour of the day here in the desert. That's what makes it so fascinating."

She went into one of the closets and brought out a luxurious eiderdown pouf to cover Cheryl for the few hours that remained of the afternoon. The change of altitude was what was making her sleepy, Mrs. Guinness said, and she could leave her unpacking until later in the day. She wanted her to be ready to enjoy the sunset which was an experience that no one should miss.

Cheryl liked sunsets, but she had never before heard anyone make such a point of them. She had seen the desert when traveling along the highway with her parents, but she'd never stayed right in the heart of it and with a household that was so geared to its moods. As sleep overcame her, she wondered what the next days would hold.

When Peter knocked on her door to awaken her, she had been so deeply asleep that she could not at first recollect where she was. A mountain outside of her window? And a Mexican tin sunburst of a mirror to reflect it? As she searched for her striped cotton pullover and ran a comb through her hair, she could no longer see the palo verde—the mountain shadows had engulfed it. Hastening out upon the terrace, she found Peter and his mother listening to organ music.

"We always play these records at this time of day because they seem to fit." Mrs. Guinness greeted her and gestured toward the mountains on the other side of the valley. Chords of color were playing across them, bright crimson on the peaks and blues below, shafts of yellow light and orange until the outlines softened with the coming of the night. "Casts a spell, doesn't it?" Mrs. Guinness murmured.

Even Peter was silent, thinking his own thoughts, perhaps, dreaming his dreams.

"You're not nearly as obnoxious as most girls I know," he said to Cheryl when later they gathered about the fireplace inside.

"Gee, thanks." Cheryl slipped a frankfurter over the stick that he had cut for her and thrust it over the flames. "Thanks a lot."

"Don't mind Peter." Mrs. Guinness had come in with the mustard and the rolls. "He takes a bit of knowing."

Cheryl leaned back with her head against a cushion. She was so comfortable here and so relaxed that Peter could have said anything to her and she wouldn't have minded—at least not tonight. She was far away from the problems that had troubled her, and here they did not seem important. The Tri Phis could have their old house party.

Peter had picked up her hand and was bending her fingers. She supposed that a girl was supposed to say "ouch," but she didn't. Peter's touch was gentle, and he wasn't hurting her.

They always went out to look at the stars before they retired, Mrs. Guinness explained, leading the way again to the terrace and to the dazzling dome of the sky overhead. Here, in the clear desert air, the constellations were magnificent—so big and so bright that you felt as though you could almost reach out and touch them. It was like this every night except at full moon, Mrs. Guinness said, adding that it was a beauty they missed in The Palisades.

"I'm always telling you we ought never to go back there, Mother," Peter reminded her. "We should stay here all the time."

"This boy would like nothing better than to join the other characters down here and become one of those no-account 'desert rats.'" Mrs. Guinness looked at her son fondly. "But his father and I have other plans for him."

"Which I haven't the slightest intention of following." Peter turned again to the constellations and began to identify them. The one that looked like some celestial and gigantic TV aerial was Orion, and the W inscribed in the sky was Cassiopeia's Chair.

"Queen of Ethiopia so beautiful the sea nymphs were jealous of her," Cheryl murmured to Peter's surprise and her own. A bit of the knowledge she had gained as a Girl Scout was coming back to her. Together they located the Big Dipper and the North Star which were the clock of the heavens and the navigator's guide, Peter said, making the stars come further alive for Cheryl. It was better than a trip to the big Los Angeles planetarium up in Griffith Park.

"I think I'll be an astronomer," Peter remarked idly as he continued his survey of the spangled canopy that twinkled above them.

"Last week you wanted to be a geologist." Mrs. Guinness laughed. "And next week?"

"Anyway, something that has nothing to do with Hollywood or any of those big corporations. I want to be myself, and not run with the pack."

"Your father makes a pretty good living at it." Mrs. Guinness defended the movie industry.

"Money isn't everything." Peter dug into one of his pockets and pulled out several dark chunks that he said were pieces of meteorites. "It's things like this that count."

Mrs. Guinness slapped at another of his pockets playfully and brought forth the jingle of coins. "How would you know about money when you've never been without it?"

"Well, you know what I mean, Mom." Peter was exasperated and rude. "Don't act so stupid."

"Yes, I do." Mrs. Guinness ran a hand through his crew cut. "Your father and I are glad that you seem to be developing a sound sense of values. See that you keep them."

Because Mrs. Guinness said that dawn was another momentous part of almost any day in the desert and that they usually rose in time to enjoy it, she suggested an early good night. "Be sure to put on something warm in the morning, my dear. It can turn very cold." She accompanied Cheryl to her room to turn down the covers. "So nice to have you here. Sleep well."

They had breakfast things packed and were waiting in the jeep by the time Cheryl got into windbreaker and jeans and sleepily laced up her high tennis shoes the next morning. Mrs. Guinness was wearing scarlet squaw boots with handsome silver buttons upon them and had offered to lend Cheryl a pair, but she preferred her old tennis shoes that nothing could harm.

As she settled upon the pillows that Mrs. Guinness insisted upon Peter's bringing to relieve the hardness of the seats, she hoped that his mother would be equally firm about the course that he took. She was not about to risk her neck again climbing any more hills.

There was a faint glow in the sky above the mountains toward which they were heading in the dusky pre-dawn light, and soon a flame of scarlet throbbed. Cheryl could see what Mrs. Guinness meant about the dramatics of dawn in the desert . . . how thrillingly the mountains stood in sharp silhouette. Every one of them could have been cut out of purplish-black felt.

Here and there, a jackrabbit leaped across ahead of them and stood with long ears quivering, watching the passage of the automotive monster in which they were riding. And occasionally, above the noise of the motor, Cheryl could hear a mournful wail that sent shivers down her spine. "Coyotes," she managed to read from Mrs. Guinness's lips.

Just as the glittering rim of the sun began to show itself, Peter stopped beside a deep gully and unloaded their gear. They could help him carry it down to the bottom of the wash, he said, trying to override his mother's objections. Peter could talk all he liked about the interesting rock specimens he hoped to find there and he could explore for them later, his mother said, but she was not about to prepare breakfast where the risk was so great. They could be caught in a raging torrent if one of the flash floods poured down from the mountains.

"The desert makes its own rules, and it's wise to observe them," she explained to Cheryl, using as a further example a thick stand of bushes beside which the girl stood. It would be smarter to gather sticks for their campfire from another location, she said, pointing to twisting tracks that converged on the thicket. They were fresh tracks, made some time during the night or early this morning, and they were sure signs of snakes that were probably rattlers.

"Hope they've all gone back home." Cheryl jumped away with an apprehensive glance over her shoulder, half-expecting to see a venomous line of them.

"Don't bother them, and they won't bother you," Peter said carelessly, pointing to wriggling marks that indicated the further presence of sidewinders. They were more dangerous than other types of rattlers because they seldom gave warning in time to avoid them, he added, tossing off this additional piece of information as casually as anyone else might mention that today was Friday. He was obviously delighted to be able to trace the night's activities by tracks that showed where desert mice had been eaten by the snakes.

So far as Cheryl could see, they were in a regular snake pit. It was small reassurance for her to be told that the reptiles usually stayed in hiding until the sun went down. Anyone but the Guinnesses would have changed their picnic spot in a hurry, but she hated to suggest it and seem like a spoilsport.

Now Peter was pursuing a huge fuzzy brown spider and, capturing it in a paper bag, he brought it over to show her. It was a tarantula. She had always heard that they were frightfully poisonous.

"Ugh," she cried, backing away into a staghorn cactus and doing little to improve her temper. Was everything in the desert lying in wait to prick you or to bite?

Mrs. Guinness, who had been unconcernedly gathering wood and starting the fire, was soon ready with bacon and eggs. "Eat plenty," she said cordially. "The desert always gives you such an appetite."

"Y-Yes," Cheryl said doubtfully, balancing her plate as she took refuge upon a huge rock. With her feet tucked up under her, she felt fairly safe. Safe, that is, until Peter gleefully pounced upon the scorpion.

14   *Easter Week Goings-On*

Peter had found the loathsome-looking creature hiding under the rock on which she was ensconced. He held it carefully while he examined the poison needle at the end of its tail.

"Good specimen for science class," he said, making a move as though to place it in the palm of Cheryl's hand.

"Take it away! I can't stand the sight of it!" Cheryl drew back in genuine terror.

"Girls—they're all alike." Peter's voice was filled with disdain. "I thought you were different."

Mrs. Guinness, who had been watching the byplay with an amused expression, came to Cheryl's defense. "Stop teasing her, Peter. I think she's doing mighty well for her first morning in the desert. Remember, she's a city girl, and she's being an awfully good sport."

Peter went away muttering something about "dames" and disappeared down the gulch. He was probably hunting for gold again, and they'd never get him out of there, his mother explained. He had heard about a lost mine somewhere up there in one of the canyons, and he was always hoping to find traces of the ore where it had been washed down in some cloudburst.

"Peter's always looking for something." Mrs. Guinness sighed and began to pack the plates back into the picnic basket.

"Do you suppose he'll ever find it?" Cheryl could tell by Mrs. Guinness's tone that she did not refer merely to his present search for gold.

"I hope so, and I hope that you do, too." Mrs. Guinness tilted Cheryl's chin and looked deep into her eyes. "Keep on taking things pretty much in your stride, as you seem to be doing here, and you'll be surprised at what fortune may hold for you. Make the most of yourself and the most of every day as it comes."

"Thank you. I'll try . . . I really will try." Cheryl sat watching a tiny bird leap from twig to twig in the thicket, picking at the scant growth of berries and clearly unmindful of the snakes lurking there. Probably they preferred mice, and she hoped so. She'd hate to see anything happen to this saucy desert wren.

When you were quiet and let your thoughts roam, you were aware of many things in the desert that had previously escaped your attention. You wondered how this frail network of fairylike flowers could ever survive in the scorching sun. You saw the small lizards darting across the sand and heard the hum of bees about the waxen yellow blooms on a cactus.

"Not enough rain this spring to bring out many of the flowers," Mrs. Guinness observed. "Sometimes the desert is carpeted with them, and it's a sight people drive miles to see."

She disappeared down the gully to try to locate the youthful prospector and left Cheryl to gaze across the wide sweep of space that, seemingly almost empty, was yet so filled with a life all its own. You couldn't have small thoughts here in this hauntingly beautiful land; they had to be large ones. What Mrs. Guinness had said had made a profound impression upon Cheryl. It was strange how a new acquaintance could be more of a guide than your parents. Perhaps it was because parents' words had grown so worn with constant use that you did not hear them so sharply.

Lost in reverie, she was startled when Peter announced his presence by dropping a load of rocks at her feet. They sparkled in the light. He must have found gold!

"You can have it." Peter kicked it to one side. "It's only a fake. They call it 'fool's gold.' "

"Like some of the people I know." The thought of Ethel Barnes popped momentarily into Cheryl's mind, but she put it aside. She was positively not going to let Ethel spoil her desert vacation.

When Mrs. Guinness went into Palm Springs on the following day to keep a luncheon engagement and suggested that Cheryl might wish to accompany her, she was surprised to find that she did not really care about going. The desert had caught hold of her imagination, and she would have quite enough of cities for the rest of the year. Besides, Peter had mentioned the remains of an Indian aqueduct up in one of the canyons, and she wanted to see it. The Indians had built it years before to bring down the waters of a mountain spring where it gushed from the rocks, and Peter said it was a great place to find bits of Indian pottery and arrowheads.

Mrs. Guinness packed a picnic lunch for them to take and left with a warning to Cheryl. It involved another of the rules of the desert which was, "Don't put your hands into any crevices above your head when you climb." Snakes could be lurking there, and it was akin to "Look before you step."

Now, as they came out into a green mountain valley, Cheryl decided that the long and arduous climb had been worth it. She cupped her hands and drank from the clear mountain spring which flowed through the valley and was filled with darting trout. Munching the water cress which Peter had gathered to go with their lunch, she settled down in the flower-filled grass with Peter's head in her lap. He had brought along a volume of poetry from which to read, and now he opened to a lovely and singularly appropriate passage from Alfred, Lord Tennyson. . . .

> "Doubted, and drowsed, nodded and slept, and saw,
>   Dreaming, a slope of land that ever grew,
>   Field after field, up to a height, the peak
>   Haze-hidden, and thereon a phantom king. . . ."

As Peter read on from *The Coming of Arthur,* she wondered whether there was any other boy in the United States of America who would spend his time on poetry when he had a girl so close to him. Most boys would "get fresh" or at least want to kiss you. She was glad that Peter held back. When a boy was not your heart's desire, you did not want the whole afternoon to be spoiled.

They were to leave tomorrow morning, Sunday, and Mrs. Guinness wanted to get a very early start. The traffic would be bumper-to-bumper later on in the day, and she wanted to avoid it, she said, giving Peter instructions for loading the station wagon on Saturday night. The jeep always remained behind in the desert —where it belonged, in Cheryl's opinion. She had not grown fond of the jeep, but it was with a sense of loss that she bade farewell to the exquisite palo verde and the stars of the desert sky.

They were making a detour to drop her off at Belmont Beach before they went on to The Palisades. Cheryl hoped her mother would be dressed up for church by the time they arrived; she wanted Mother to appear at her most attractive. As the car rounded the familiar corners leading to Canterbury Knolls, she could hardly wait to see her. Mother always said that, for her, the best part of any trip was getting home again, and now Cheryl could see what she meant. She had been away for less than four days, but going to the desert had been such a change that it could have been weeks.

Leaving her mother, who looked lovely, and Mrs. Guinness inside making polite conversation, she took Peter out to the garage to meet her father. It was so good to feel his arms around her again, so wonderful to be home that she loved the whole world and everything in it.

She hoped that she had left her old drab self behind her forever. She sparkled all that day and all the next when she went back to her classes. From all reports, her vacation had been so much more successful than Judy's or Alicia's that they were envious of her. The weather at the shore had been cold and windy, they said, and they had wandered about practically frozen to death. Together with the other pledges, they had cooked meals and washed dishes and had had to do all the work while the older girls played.

"I call it a heck of a way to run a house party," Judy blurted out, and Alicia agreed. It had been a case of orders to do this and do that the whole while; they grew so tired of it finally they hadn't even stayed out the week. Alicia's father had come down to get them, and all the parents of pledges had been highly indignant.

"You didn't miss a thing, believe me." Alicia summed it all up for Cheryl. "If it wouldn't make a dreadful stink, I'd back out of Tri Phi right now."

"Me, too," Judy cried. "I'm sick of being treated like the dirt under somebody's feet."

When you had a glow inside of you, it showed outside, too. Everyone was talking about how well Cheryl looked . . . what a gorgeous tan she'd acquired. Judy and Alicia were insisting that the change in her must be because she was in love with Peter Guinness. She could let them think that this was the reason. It was easier than explaining what was hard to put into words . . . how free she had felt in the desert, how far from this narrow world of high school and Tri Phi.

Peter and his mother, between them, had shown her a refreshingly wider horizon, had given her glimpses of another way to live. Organ music and sunsets, poetry and mountain meadows. . . .

As the week passed, she found herself remembering each of the various aspects of her desert visit. Perhaps she should try to get up early in the mornings and see what dawn was like in Canterbury Knolls. Dew on the grass, birds singing . . . it was such a beautiful time of day, she thought, looking out of the window the next morning. She'd dress quietly, so as not to wake up her parents, and have it all to herself.

"You sick or something, dear?" Mother opened her bedroom door a crack and peered at her sleepily.

"Nope, just crazy, that's all." Cheryl skipped on outside. That was the word for it—crazy. She hadn't been so happy, really, since she could remember. For the sheer joy of it, she turned cartwheels all the way down the driveway. Let the neighbors think she was crazy if they liked, if any of them were up early enough to see her . . . a great girl cavorting on the lawn.

"I'm sure I don't know what's got into you, Cheryl—but, whatever it is, let's keep it." Mother was dumbfounded to come into the kitchen later on and find Cheryl fixing the breakfast. Coffee in the percolator was sending a delicious aroma through the house, and the table was set with a centerpiece of freshly cut roses.

"Don't expect this every morning, Mother. I wouldn't want to spoil you." Cheryl slipped bread into the toaster and commenced a hunt for the marmalade. Refreshed by her early morning gymnastics, she had pink cheeks and eyes that sparkled.

"I wouldn't know you for the same girl," Mother said, watching her.

"Can't have the muley-grubs forever, Mom." Cheryl turned on the radio and did a few dance steps around the kitchen with the dachshund for partner. Mrs. Guinness had advised her to make the most of every day, and she was practicing this to the fullest this morning.

"We must send you to the desert oftener," Mother observed. "I liked Mrs. Guinness immensely, and I hope she liked me."

"Why wouldn't she? Don't you get along pretty well with almost everybody?"

"That's my girl." Father appeared to share in the general good spirits that were unusual in the Kramer household at this time of day.

Cheryl had taken time to put up her hair the previous

night. Now, when she went into the bathroom to comb it, each curl fell in place. When she didn't wait to get up until the last possible minute and gave herself plenty of time, things went more smoothly. She could be pleased with her appearance, for a change, and not rush off to school only half put together.

As she slipped a fresh pink cotton dress over her newly starched petticoat and reached for the zipper, she frowned at her shoes. She'd forgotten all about them last night when she made her other preparations. She should have shined them. When would Cheryl Kramer ever have the brains to remember every last little, but very important, detail? That would be the day . . . sometime in May.

She hummed a tune to go along with the words . . . sometime in May . . . as she tripped on toward school with her petticoat swaying about her. Bill Meyers was going to address the high school assembly today, and she wanted to be at her best for this special occasion. Sophomores and their parents were to hear a talk and demonstration based upon the extracurricular activities offered by Hunterford High which would be followed by refreshments in the school cafeteria. Bill and other prominent juniors were scheduled to be on hand there to answer questions, and Cheryl had a string of them. Now, for the first time, she'd be able to introduce herself to Bill Meyers. Now she had a legitimate excuse to talk with him.

As she settled in her balcony seat in the school auditorium, being careful not to wrinkle her skirt, Cheryl decided her shoes didn't matter. If she were as fortunate as she hoped she would be, she'd have him looking into her eyes—he was exactly the height for it. And, since Mother had not been able to accept the invitation to attend the assembly, she'd be free to pursue her carefully laid plans.

So far as Cheryl was concerned, there was only one extracurricular activity in which she was interested, and that was Bill Meyers. Except for Bill, who was acting as master of ceremonies, the program was tiresomely long. Who cared about the school band playing "Stars and Stripes Forever" when cake-and-punch time was waiting? Or about the boys' and girls' chorus followed by several duets and solo numbers? She'd seen the school tumblers several times previously, and she knew how the art class went about making posters.

Bill was doing his best to keep things moving, but, to the restless girl in the balcony, the program was lasting forever. She doodled on her copy of the high school paper, just off the press, without bothering to read it. Her eyes were fixed upon the stage and upon the central figure whom she had long worshipped from afar.

When finally the drama group finished a scene from the most recent high school play and the program came to its close, she prepared to make a dash for refreshments. Along the way she was stopped by one of the teachers who wanted her to assist with the serving, and she accepted joyfully. Bill could see how helpful and efficient she was, and she'd slice him an extra large piece of cake. It would be a conversational opening, and she would make the most of it, she thought, as her plans spun about in her head.

Better yet, she would give him a choice of several kinds of cake and bring them to him with a fork and a napkin. Surveying the array on the table before her, she decided upon chocolate with nuts, strawberry icing, coconut frosted, and caramel fudge. How clever Bill would think her, and how considerate of his pleasure!

She kept one eye on the door and the other on the cakes as she proceeded to cut them. The room was filled with parents and students, but the master of ceremonies was slow to appear. Perhaps, after all her scheming, he had decided to skip this last, and most significant, part of the whole afternoon affair.

She had almost given up hope when she glimpsed him through the shifting throng; he was paying attention only to the girl who clung to his arm. Knife still upraised, Cheryl froze where she stood. Ethel Barnes was twittering up at him, and he was looking at her adoringly.

"Would you think they'd have to be so public about it?" The girl next to Cheryl gave a forthright opinion. "I think it's disgusting."

"Are—are they going steady?" Cheryl tried to keep the quaver out of her voice.

"Didn't you read about it in the high school paper?" The girl opened her copy and pointed to the place on page two. There, in plain black print which Cheryl could scarcely read for the tears that filled her eyes, was the whole story. It had all happened down at the shore during Easter week, and it had first position in the chatty gossip column:

Newest Snuggle-Bunnies, Bill Meyers and Ethel Barnes, were seen cuddling mighty close. Could have been the weather—could be. But guess what Ethel found in her Easter basket. A fraternity pin!

15 *Giving*

Why hadn't Judy and Alicia told her about what was going on? They must have known all the while and kept it to themselves. Maybe that was one of the reasons they had been so cross about the whole house party—they knew how Cheryl felt about Bill and didn't want Ethel to snare him. Best friends didn't care to be first with bad news, and it would come out all too soon anyway.

Cheryl was staggered by the impact of it. She could not endure having to stay here and watch the two Snuggle-Bunnies together. Saying that she did not feel well and asking the other servers to please finish cutting the cakes, she dashed out of the building.

Some girls had all the luck—and had it in spades—and others had none. Life was so unfair that she was running away blindly. "Better watch it, miss," a traffic cop shouted after her as she fled on unseeing, not watching the lights. "You want to get killed?"

Cheryl slowed down then, but only because she was panting for breath. What difference would it make whether a person got killed and had to leave a world in which girls like Ethel Barnes got every single thing that they wanted? What was the use of trying to live in it and be happy when every single thing went against you?

She thought of what her mother often said—that Cheryl wanted things too hard. Perhaps her mother was right. Maybe what a person should do was turn into a vegetable. Be a person with no more feelings nor desires than a cabbage or a carrot.

As Cheryl hurried on, scarcely conscious of where she was going, she hadn't noticed that she had unintentionally walked down the street where Feeney lived. Feeney was the last person on earth she wanted to encounter today, but chances were that she would not run into her. Feeney had more than likely stayed on at school to get her share of refreshments.

"Yoo-hoo." It was too late to turn back now that Feeney was in the car that slowed down beside her. "I knew it was you when you turned the corner, and I told Mother to hurry."

Feeney got out with a big load of groceries. "We're going to have a barbecue tonight, and couldn't you stay for it?"

"Yes, do." Mrs. Chase seconded her daughter's invitation. "I was just saying to Feeney that I wished we had a guest to share it with us. She's told me so much about you that I'll be happy for the chance to get better acquainted."

"I—uh—well—uh—" Cheryl's mind was still in such a turmoil that she could think of no excuse to refuse. Besides, even a barbecue with Feeney and her family would be better than going straight home to cry her heart out.

"My, what a pretty dress! I wish I had one like it." Feeney fluttered about, dusting off one of the patio chairs to make sure that Cheryl didn't add further soil to the skirt that was already smudged with a bit of cake frosting. "You always have such pretty clothes, Cheryl."

"Perhaps you can help us decide what to buy Feeney for summer." Mrs. Chase's eyes twinkled pleasantly at Cheryl behind glasses with severe tortoise-shell rims. "I understand that your mother is a model. You should know the very latest."

Maybe she should, but she didn't, usually. "I don't pay as much attention as Mother says I ought to," Cheryl admitted.

She thought of how messy she customarily looked in contrast with Ethel. Today had been an exception, but it had been too late to do her the slightest bit of good. It wasn't that she didn't have nice clothes to wear, but that she didn't take care of them properly and didn't stand straight.

Still, it was refreshing to bask in admiration for a change and be asked for advice. Should Feeney cut her ponytail or shouldn't she? Was blue a good color for her or should she wear red?

"Red." Cheryl said it with a certain conviction. Feeney was such a drab little thing that red might help her stand out from the crowd. Red or orange, and her dark silky hair was probably best in a ponytail. Clearly, Mrs. Chase in her flat-heeled oxfords was a person with "no style at all," as Mother would say, but apparently she had many other interests. As they came through the house, Cheryl had noticed many well-filled book shelves and an array of musical instruments.

She had heard Feeney mention in an offhand way that she played the guitar. Now, when Cheryl asked her about it, she brought out an instrument beautifully inlaid with mother-of-pearl and strummed a few chords.

"Want to sing 'The E-ri-e' with me?"

Cheryl shook her head. Alicia was rather familiar with folk music, but all that Cheryl knew about it was that she enjoyed it on television. Now she rocked with the rhythm as Feeney began:

> "We were forty miles from Albany,
>   Forget it I never shall,
>   What a terrible storm we had one night
>   On the E-ri-e Canal."

Feeney was really good! Cheryl clapped her hands and cried for more of Feeney's repertoire. The girl barely stroked the strings of the guitar as she began another, more poignant, refrain:

"Love, oh, love, oh careless love,
   Love, oh, love, oh careless love,
It's love, oh, love, oh, careless love,
   You see what love has done for me."

As Feeney finished the sad little ballad with, "Oh, it's done and broke this heart of mine . . . and it'll break that heart of yours some time," Cheryl fought to hold back her tears. Feeney had touched a sensitive nerve, and she had given a profoundly moving performance.

With that beautiful voice of hers, she ought to be in the girls' chorus up at high school. And if not, why not? Cheryl was discovering a lot about Feeney that she hadn't suspected. Feeney had been too shy to try out for the chorus, she learned, but she might get up enough courage to do it next fall.

"If you don't, I'll make you." Cheryl was firm about that. What a shame to have Feeney hiding all of this talent when other girls with not half her ability were getting all the applause. She and Feeney had more in common than she had ever supposed in their casual lunch-hour contacts. She and Feeney were alike in that they were sitting back and letting other girls run off with all of the prizes.

"It means a lot to Feeney to have you for a friend." Mrs. Chase had come out in time to catch the last part of their talk. "You must see more of each other."

"I think we will." Cheryl said it slowly, measuring each one of her words. "I really think that we will."

It was not long after her evening with the Chases that Cheryl's mother announced at the dinner table that she had been asked to start a kind of charm school for the Girls' Club in North Belmont Beach. Cheryl had been only half-listening to her mother's general discussion of this new venture with her father, and she spoke without thinking. "Don't look at me," she said.

Mother had been saying something about poor girls who needed help, and Cheryl's mind was far from this subject unless it might apply to herself. "Charity begins at home" . . . that might be what Mother was talking about. She decided to pay closer attention, and she was surprised when Mother greeted her idle remark with an outburst.

"Good heavens, Cheryl, we try to do everything for you, and many of these girls have nothing at all. Sometimes I'm ashamed of you."

Well, what had she done now? Really, what had she done? She'd barely opened her mouth, and here Mother was about to go into one of her tempers. Cheryl had been woolgathering and as little concerned with North Belmont Beach as with the North Pole.

"I was asking you to assist me, Cheryl, and that's all the answer I get."

Father smoothed things over by asking Mother to start from the beginning and go straight through to the end. Mother had a way of jumping about in her conversation sometimes, and he wasn't too clear, either, about the whole project.

"It's like this . . ." Mother started to explain with ill-concealed impatience. She'd been talking about nothing else the whole dinnertime, and someone around here should have listened to her, she said. What the Charity League was asking of her was to set aside part of Thursday afternoons for the Girls' Club. She wouldn't be doing it for money but as part of community service. And, without Cheryl's help, it would be altogether too much for her.

"But what can I do, Mom?" Cheryl was surprised that Mother should thus count upon her.

"Lots of things. I think that most people are altogether too selfish, and this is a chance for us to extend ourselves. We Kramers can do something."

"About what?"

Cheryl listened attentively as her mother went into a long discussion of juvenile delinquency and the effect of broken homes. Girls were going wrong because they had no one to guide them and no inspiration. They lived in dreary apartments or housing projects, and they had little in their lives but poverty and even violence and crime.

North Belmont Beach was the most dismal section of the city, and Cheryl had seldom so much as driven through it. It was not as colorful as the part of downtown Los Angeles she had seen on the day she took the bus, but Mother said that the same social forces were at work in North Belmont Beach and that they dragged people down to the depths.

"Giving part of Thursday afternoons is little enough one can do to help," Mother finished, and Father agreed with her. He'd prepare dinner on Thursdays so that Mother could take it easy when she arrived home. This was a family project, and the Kramers were in it together. It was almost like marching with flags, Cheryl thought, as she went off to bed that night determined to carry one.

The girls who were to come to the charm school in the Girls' Club building were all from junior high schools in the vicinity, and they would be looking up to Cheryl as an example, Mother had said. It was a new thought for Cheryl to be an example to anyone, least of all to a crowd of girls who were almost her age. She'd better start practicing immediately so that, when the time came, she'd not disappoint them. Mother was going to teach them things like proper carriage and general cleanliness and making the most of what you had.

There it was again . . . making the most of yourself. Could Cheryl never escape it? Perhaps she couldn't because it was one thing that any girl could do. Whether she lived in Canterbury Knolls or in North Belmont Beach, she could do the best she could with what she had.

And what should she wear to the first Girls' Club session? Mother suggested that a "Before" and "After" sequence might be an excellent idea, and together they planned it. The "Before" would be simple. Slightly exaggerated, it would be the way Cheryl too often went off to high school. Run-over heels and unpolished shoes . . . a sweater she was wearing one more time when it ought to have been washed . . . ditto for her blouse . . . and a skirt that sagged down in the back.

"Come in with a slump," Mother advised, and that, too, was easy for Cheryl. She'd no need to rehearse what was a daily occurrence. What she needed some work on was the "After" routine.

When Mother picked her up at high school for their first afternoon at the Girls' Club, Cheryl was giggling. Judy and Alicia had devised a card for Mother to place upon the stage; it said, with enormous question marks, WHAT DO YOU KNOW???

"Glad to see that your friends take such an interest," Mother said, putting the card in the backseat along with other props she expected to use.

"Why, they're absolutely popping. They wanted to come along with us."

"Another time." Mother drove along thoughtfully. "This isn't exactly entertainment, you know."

Standing in the wings and watching the girls march into the small auditorium, Cheryl felt her heart go out to every one of them. As she told Judy and Alicia later, you couldn't see them without being ashamed of yourself for ever complaining. They were trying so hard to be beautiful, and they were so very pathetic. You could pass a few such girls on the street scarcely noticing, as she often had, but to see a crowd of them together was an entirely different affair.

They were trying with elaborate cosmetics to cover up for the poor clothes that they wore. Dripping mascara . . . lipstick that made hideous gashes out of young pretty mouths . . . foundation cream masks . . . all this and more supported an air of bravado.

Right from the beginning, Mother let them have it. "What are you hiding under all that stuff? Wrinkles? Wait until you're my age, and you'll have to worry about that."

She carried them along with her by making fun of herself. "And who needs to be a blonde? Leave that to me. What's wrong with keeping your hair in its natural color? Remember that Cleopatra, the siren of the Nile, was brunette."

She went on into the proper care of complexions and of hair. "Washing, washing with plain soap and water. That will do more for you and your looks than any fancy foundations or any hair dyes you find. Don't try to grow up too fast . . . you're young, young, YOUNG. I wish I were," she added in an aside that made the girls laugh and brought Cheryl out on the stage.

"Is this the way you leave for school every morning? Who said you couldn't wash your blouse and your sweater? That's the difference between a lady and a tramp. And I'm sure you all want to be ladies. . . . Now go back and change." She explained that Cheryl was her daughter, and that was why she could order her around though she didn't always obey her.

To give Cheryl time to emerge in her "After" guise, Mrs. Kramer went into a line of patter about mothers and daughters that brought grins from her audience. They knew that she understood them, but she was being so gay and spontaneous about it that she was giving no offense.

When Cheryl returned in a similar outfit but one

which was clean and well pressed, they applauded her until Mother resumed. "You see how simple it is? Just a matter of a little soap and water and a little extra time. Anybody who has a blouse can wash it. One blouse is as good as a dozen, and the same with one pair of panties."

Afterward, the girls crowded around to ask questions —all sorts of them. Mother had only begun the lessons of the charm school, but apparently the girls simply loved it. Mother hadn't exactly scolded them, but she had made certain points.

"I do hope they'll stick. A little bit, anyway." As Mother started back to Canterbury Knolls, she was not sure of her ultimate success, nor was Cheryl. When you had such a little to work with, as so many of these girls apparently did, how could you expect much improvement?

Cheryl had more clothes than she needed, and perhaps she could share them. She'd ask Judy and Alicia and other friends, too, she decided in a rush of enthusiasm.

"And so where would you start?" Mother smiled at her generosity. "You wouldn't have enough to give something to everyone, would you?"

16   *A New Cheryl*

"The need among those girls is so great that all we can do is to give them a bit of ourselves. Show that somebody cares," Mother said, being realistic instead of sentimental.

As the weeks passed on toward the latter part of spring, Cheryl became more and more engrossed in the Girls' Club. She baked cupcakes and cookies so that there would be enough to serve to all of the girls. Mother was teaching them how to carry on a conversation, and the regular class was now followed by a social event.

Without realizing it, Cheryl was changing her attitude toward herself as well as toward others now that she was practicing good grooming every day of the week. If she didn't follow her own mother's advice, what could they expect of the girls? Fingernails didn't become neat and well-shaped overnight; her complexion wouldn't stay clear unless she scrubbed it daily with liquid green soap and watched what she ate. Mother was telling the girls that, if they had a dime to spend, to look for an apple instead of a chocolate bar.

Toothpaste did not cost much, nor did deodorant; and young girls could find greater beauty in sparkling white teeth than in the most expensive cosmetics. "Keep it clean, and I do mean yourselves," was one of Mother's favorite punch lines, and she repeated it over and over.

Naturally Cheryl had to practice what Mother preached, and many of the girls were doing likewise. They adored Mother and sought her approval. As the weeks passed, more and more of them were slowly coming into bloom.

"Keep it simple" was another watchword that was having its effect. Frizzy, exaggerated hairdos were disappearing; blouses with gewgaws on them were going the way of shoddy artificial flowers and teetering high heels and prints worn with plaids.

When her mother was busy in other directions, the girls turned to Cheryl to answer their problems. If you were going to earn fifty cents doing ironing for a neighbor lady, how would you spend it? What do you do when a boy gets fresh? When your best friend says nasty things about you, should you call her a liar? How can you keep the cops from pestering you when you haven't done anything wrong?

Cheryl put her arm around the girl who had asked the last question and drew her aside. She was a pretty little thing, big-eyed and wistful, like a French waif in a movie magazine photograph. Her brother was a thief. Cheryl longed to take her home with her and make everything right, but she knew Mother would say that this was beyond them. All they could do was to be kind to girls like this and to others who appeared weary-eyed because they had been up all night trying to keep fathers from beating mothers in some alcoholic nightmare.

Cheryl was hearing many stories that shocked her and shocked Mother. Life was so grim for some of these girls that you wondered how they could ever summon the courage to smile. How small Cheryl's own problems appeared when she compared them with theirs! She was so busy thinking about these other girls that she hadn't been sorry for herself in weeks.

Here was the case of the girl whom the others considered to be a real heiress. Her grandmother had died and left her twenty-seven dollars and fifty cents. Imagine having a grandmother who thought that much of you and had that much to give! She could buy a whole wardrobe with such a magnificent sum, the class thought, and Mother made it a project. They were all to shop around during the week, price various articles, and come up with suggestions.

Seldom had there been such excitement at the sessions

as when, on the following Thursday, the girls reported what they'd discovered. One had found an orlon bulky at a bargain three-ninety-five, another for five-ninety-five, and so it went through skirts and blouses and shoes.

"Will it pay her to buy the cheapest or the best?" Mother insisted that every girl decide for herself and make her own recommendations.

Several of them insisted that she could buy more clothes if she chose the cheap ones, and that's what they'd do with this much money. But others disagreed. "Cheap things fall apart," they said, telling of various sorry experiences. "Cheap things don't look nice very long."

To put the whole matter up to a vote, Mother made two signs and attached them to the draperies on either side of the room. One said CHEAP, and the other spelled QUALITY which meant clothes with seams that wouldn't pull apart the first time you wore them, shoes that didn't have paper soles, labels that guaranteed this fabric would shrink very little . . . things like that.

When the majority of the girls trooped over to stand under the QUALITY sign, Mother beamed. They were learning, she said, and she was so happy about it that she was going to tell them about a special surprise. "We're going to have a fashion show, and everyone's going to be in it. You can invite your mothers to a parade of spring and summer fashions from Bunting's Department Store."

From the hubbub which arose at her announcement, one would think that Mother was about to offer them the sun, moon, and stars. New clothes! A chance to be a real fashion model! Next week Cheryl would show them how to walk and how to carry themselves properly, her mother continued, glaring Cheryl to silence.

This was the first the girl had heard about this angle of the show, and she was sure it was her mother's way of forcing her to do more work on herself. "The way you wear your clothes is as important as what you wear." That had long been one of her mother's dictums that Cheryl had been slow to obey. "Shoulders and head high—pull in your stomach—don't look at your feet."

While her mother was busying herself taking down sizes and measurements, Cheryl noticed that one of the girls had picked up a small ceramic figure from the corner desk where it stood and, thinking that no one was observing her, slipped it into her purse. Mother had told her that something of this sort might happen, and that she was to keep a watchful eye at all times; but that she was not to embarrass the wrongdoer in front of the rest.

Now the girl was leaving for the washroom, and Cheryl followed her. "That's a mighty big purse you have," Cheryl said by way of opening the conversation tactfully. "I expect you can carry a lot in it."

"You saw me! I know you did." The girl sobbed, hiding her face in her arms. "And you're going to turn me into the cops."

She had taken the figure because it was pretty, she wailed. She only wanted something pretty to have in her room. Cheryl could picture how drab it must be.

"I've got something you'll like even better." Cheryl thought of the two musical powderboxes she'd been given last Christmas. One was blue and one was pink, and each had a ballerina that danced on its top. She had no use for two of them, anyway. "If you'll put back what you took right where you found it, I'll bring you a present next week. Don't you tell anybody either . . . we'll keep it a secret."

She returned to the auditorium to find her mother trying to keep her wits about her amidst the general consternation. Taking sizes had set off a furor because some of the girls were not at all sure about theirs and were ashamed to admit it. Apparently, all the clothes they had were hand-me-downs where the question of size was settled with safety pins. Mrs. Kramer was having a difficult time reassuring them that they didn't have to inform her; she could judge fairly well just by looking at them, and they needn't worry one bit.

There were other girls who, on second thought, were getting cold feet about the whole idea of the show. Several were dumpy and said they knew they'd look awful, while others didn't like the thought of undressing and dressing in front of the rest. Likely they were sensitive about their ragged underclothing.

Feminine pride and feminine temperaments were threatening to take over when Mother closed the session firmly with, "None of us is perfect, remember that. We can only do the best that we can. Now, if there's any girl here who thinks she is perfect, will she please raise her hand?" The audience sat motionless.

Several of the girls followed Cheryl and her mother to their car to continue their clamor, but Mother would have no more of it. "See you next week," she said, getting into the car and driving away.

"It's going to be an awfully big job to put on that show, isn't it?" Cheryl sighed as she settled back in her seat.

"You can say that again. I wish I'd never thought of it." Mother was keyed up as she reviewed the situation.

On Saturday, she and Cheryl would go to Bunting's and talk to the buyers in the various departments, Mother planned. If the store had a high school shop, that would make it simple. Because it didn't, Cheryl and Mother would have to search through the store for clothes that were inexpensive but good—and which were suitable for girls of this age. What Mrs. Kramer had promised the store management was to demonstrate how girls could dress attractively upon limited means. It was a difficult assignment that she had set for herself and for Cheryl.

Bunting's was eager to have her do it as an experiment, she explained. They were interested in appealing to folk in the lower-income brackets and would give her the run of the store. "And every one of those girls will be jealous of the next one if we don't watch out what we give her to wear," Mother finished wearily.

To give themselves plenty of time, Cheryl and her mother started out right after breakfast. Next Saturday they would finish up the rest of the details, and that would have to be that. They had only the two days in which to outfit forty-odd girls, and Mother said she must have been insane to have thought it was possible.

As Cheryl followed her mother through Bunting's to the sportswear department, which seemed a good place to start, she thought she caught a glimpse of Bill Meyers disappearing into one of the stock rooms. He had become such a mirage in her life that she couldn't be sure. Besides, what difference did it make? Now that he was going steady with Ethel, she had abandoned all hopes. She was not about to run through all the nooks and crannies of a store to try to encounter Bill Meyers.

Mother was impatient and telling her to hurry, please. They didn't have all day to linger at the scarf counter where Cheryl had stopped to stare at the door which had slammed closed behind the youth, whoever he might be. As they went on to examine the colorful pieces of sportswear, she stood obediently while Mother held them up to her.

"Full skirts are best to conceal figure defects," the buyer suggested, adding hastily, "not that your daughter has them. I mean the other girls you have told me about. Your daughter has a perfectly beautiful figure."

She couldn't have said the same thing about me a few months ago, Cheryl thought, none the less grateful for the compliment. She had thinned down considerably. One of her three wishes had come true, even if the others would never be granted.

"And such good taste in clothes," the buyer continued, admiring Cheryl's outfit. "You must be very proud of her," she told Mother.

"I am—sometimes—in fact, most of the time now-adays." Mother continued chatting with the buyer while they awaited a new shipment that was coming in from the price-marking room. The buyer had a pleasant personality, but she seemed pushed by the pressures of department store life. Now she went to the house phone and was sharp with someone at the other end of the line.

"Told him to hurry up," she said. "That new stock boy isn't as quick as he might be." She muttered something about part-time store trainees and how you never could count on "these high school kids."

"I'm one," Cheryl said, resenting the remark. Whoever the boy was, she felt the need to defend him. Teenagers were no worse and no slower than anyone else.

"Sorry, no offense intended." The buyer tapped her pencil while she awaited the results of her phone call.

Presently, a large cart appeared down the aisle impelled by some force that was, as yet, invisible. "The boy's so awkward I hope he doesn't bang the counters with it." The buyer raised her voice so that he'd be sure to overhear her.

Cheryl was curious to find out who it was that was incurring her wrath. She saw two long arms emerge upon either side of the cart and then a long, bent body struggling to turn it around a difficult corner.

"Well, you finally made it, I see." The buyer scolded as Bill Meyers drew himself to full height and meekly proceeded to unload the various garments. "Better late than never."

Bill shrugged his shoulders and said nothing. When

he had finished, he was about to walk away when the buyer told him to "stick around." She could never find him when she needed him, she said, and she had another job for him when "these ladies" had finished their selections. She indicated Cheryl and her mother.

Bill watched them idly. Apparently, they were only two ordinary customers so far as he was concerned. But, as the pile in front of Cheryl grew, he showed a sudden interest.

"Is your mother buying all these clothes for you?"

"Why, sure. I'm only going to wear each outfit once and then throw it away." A foolish question deserved a silly answer, and Cheryl could see no point in trying to make a special impression upon Bill when he already belonged to Ethel. If she were the kind of girl whom he liked . . . if he went for her type in a great big enormous way. . . .

"Say, haven't I seen you around somewhere before?" He brushed back the lock of hair that had strayed down over his eyes and looked at her with an intensity that, under other circumstances, would have thrilled her clear down to her toes.

"Could be. I've been around Hunterford High all this year." She was not about to tell him that she was aware that he was a big man on campus or even that she knew his name.

"I'm Bill Meyers. And you're—"

"Cheryl Kramer. The 'Z' is silent as in zebra."

"Great sense of humor . . . really great." He grinned at her in the way she had known Bill would do—slow and easy—with his eyes as well as his mouth. He warmed up all over. "Now tell me why you're here and what you're doing."

As she explained to him about the Girls' Club and about the fashion show, it was astonishingly simple for her to relax and feel natural. She had always thought that the first time she met him she'd be sure to have stage fright, yet here she was able to be her very own self.

Perhaps the knowledge that she looked extremely well today was part of it. Perhaps it was because she wasn't always worrying now about what other people thought of her; she had lost some of her self-consciousness. And it could be also because she was thinking about the girls at the Club more than about herself— she wanted Bill to understand all about them.

By the time the buyer was ready to have Bill put the clothes she and Mother had chosen on a special rack and wheel them back to the stock room for later delivery, Cheryl was doing most of the talking. Bill was listening to her attentively.

"Yeh, it's tough for those kids . . . most of 'em don't have a chance. Nice to meet somebody who's trying to do something for them. I've had boys like that in summer camp and. . . ." He waved back at her from the cart. "See you around somewhere, maybe."

"Like next Saturday. We'll be back here again." There, that hadn't sounded so very bold, had it?

"I must say you're a great help, Cheryl. Spending your time with that boy just when I needed you most."

Mother was trying to sound cross, but she didn't succeed. "Can't say I blame you, though. He's very nice looking."

"Do you really think so, Mom?" Cheryl hoped she sounded as matter-of-fact as she was attempting to feel. She couldn't start to dream about Bill all over again when her dreams hadn't the slightest chance of coming true.

"Yes, I do. Much more your type than Peter Guinness. Your father and I rather liked Peter . . . thought he was interesting . . . but. . . ."

"But what, Mom?"

"But nothing. We've other things to do today than have a heart-to-heart talk, haven't we?"

"I guess so." In a way, it was a relief to Cheryl to have so many other things on her mind.

17   *"Let's Give It a Try."*

"Oh, what a muddle!" There were a good many times during the rest of this Saturday and the one that followed when Cheryl and her mother all but despaired. At times it seemed well nigh impossible to find attractive clothes that would suit forty Club members of every size, shape and coloring—and still keep within prices the girls could afford. If they were at all extravagant, they'd discourage the girls and send them back to wearing only what was tawdry and cheap.

Yet it was a case of "the show must go on"; neither

Cheryl nor her mother disagreed about that. The girls
were counting on it, however reluctant some had appeared; they must not be disappointed. These were
girls who had been let down far too often in the course
of their lives. What Mother was trying to do, with
Cheryl's aid, was to make her small part of it fair and
good. No, the Kramers could not add to the long list of
hurts and betrayals. Cheryl felt this more deeply than
her mother, perhaps; she knew how deeply things could
cut you when you were young even if you had a good
home and parents who loved and protected you.

The afternoon preceding the show was dress rehearsal. When the girls were finally dressed and lined up to
go onstage and practice their turns, Cheryl was completely exhausted. Jealousies raged all about her, and it
was useless for Mother to have warned her a dozen
times in the past few days that this was to be fully expected. "Whatever they say, don't take it personally. It's
part of their basic insecurity. Remember that."

Despite the fact that Mother had brought along
scarves and belts and beads to glamorize the simpler outfits, many of the girls were discontented and accused the
Kramers of playing favorites. All of the girls were
prickly and nervous. Mrs. Kramer did her best to calm
them, but some were close to hysteria when she finally
sent them off with last-minute instructions which em-
phasized the cleanliness which was the basic part of
being well dressed. No girl could be in the show unless
she had taken a bath and used a deodorant.

"They'd just better!" Cheryl thought crossly, thinking of all the last-minute details that still lay ahead. It would be hours before she and her mother were ready to leave.

Yet the next afternoon—as the mothers began to file into the small auditorium along with aunts and a few fathers, and all the girls milled about her backstage— Cheryl forgot the hours of work that had led to this moment and abandoned herself to the rising tide of excitement. Loading the record player with the music that would accompany the show, she breathed a short prayer.

Her grandmother might not have approved of this time and place, but it was a prayer all the same. And it was a prayer about people—about girls with pimples and shining eyes, about girls with flat chests and those with full bosoms, about shy girls and bold ones, about girls everywhere. *Give them their dreams,* her prayer said, *give them their dreams.*

And then the strains of "The Blue Danube" floated out across the auditorium, and the show was ready to start. Mother stepped out in front to give her welcoming speech and do the commentating. From now on whatever happened behind the scenes was up to Cheryl.

She was so busy buttoning buttons, zipping zippers, buckling belts that she had no further time to think. As she flew about her various tasks, she could hear the ripple of applause that greeted the girls as each self-consciously took her place in the limelight. Walking across the stage was a real effort for many of them, but Cheryl could see that their faces were glowing as they descended from the stage to sit in a special section with an impressive sign over it which said RESERVED FOR FASHION SHOW MODELS.

It was as much of a thrill for Cheryl as it was for the girls to know that the show was making a hit. The mothers were loving it and laughing in all the right places. Mrs. Kramer had added witty comments here and there to enliven the pace; and, as she stood there so poised and so smart in her white sharkskin suit, one daughter's heart was nearly bursting with pride. It was really Mother's show, Cheryl thought. As she stood beside her to take a bow when it ended, Cheryl felt she had tiny right to the hearty applause.

Afterward, darting about to serve the refreshments, she had a chance to talk to some of the mothers. They were so friendly and enthusiastic and grateful that she was almost embarrassed. Anyone would think that the Kramers had done a great thing with their charm school to judge by what the mothers were saying. "My daughter's a different girl." . . . "She lives for Thursday afternoons." . . . Comments like that.

Every single one of them wanted to buy what her daughter had modeled, and the girls were flitting here and there like so many twittering birds. Some of them could go straight home in their pretty new outfits, while others had to be consoled with Bunting's layaway plan.

Mrs. Kramer was busy taking orders and accepting down payments, with Cheryl's assistance. In the end, no one was to be disappointed, as Cheryl and her mother had planned. They had held a family conference only this morning, and Father had suggested that they could quietly finance a few of the girls if their families seemed unable to afford a new outfit. "It's the least we can do," Father had said as he left for his office.

Fashion shows were practically never a "sellout" as this one had been, Mother said to Cheryl as she steered away into the sunset and wondered aloud what Father might be preparing for dinner. She'd go down to Bunting's first thing in the morning to tell them about it. They would be so delighted they would practically be ready to offer her the whole store. "Or want us to do another show for the Girls' Club right away." Mother groaned to Cheryl's ready accompaniment.

Their charm school was soon to close for the summer. As Mother talked about it several days later, Cheryl felt a real sense of loss. She had come to count upon Thursday afternoons because it had made her feel good to be helping somebody else. The activity had taken her away from her own problems. Now she'd have to face them again.

The prospect of the long summer stretching before her was not an enticing one. After the first few days of vacation, she would have little to occupy her unless she attended summer school. Long days on the lawn or at the beach could become a crashing bore unless a girl had a beau. Other summers, it had been fun to laze around on the beach with a bunch of other girls, but this year was different. It had been different ever since mid-September when she'd gone into high school.

Recently, Cheryl had gotten out of her old habit of

feeling sorry for herself, but it would be easy to slip back into her old ways if she thought too much about the summer and the fall that would follow. She would go back to school as a junior; she had failed to make a sorority and, so far as she could see, it would be the same dreary old grind. High marks, perhaps . . . low social life. In her opinion, going back to school would be like eating oatmeal; you went because it was said to be good for you.

Now, as though to add to her distress, her mother was talking about a dance for the Girls' Club. The girls would invite their boyfriends, and it would be a lovely way to end the whole season. What had started Mother off on this tangent was Bunting's suggestion that she might like to make use of some of their spring window decorations. Mother had leaped on from there to the idea of a dance as important to social development.

So far as the girls at the Club were concerned, this was all well and good. But what was Cheryl supposed to do about getting a partner? It was a very large BUT in her mind. The girls would expect her to appear with some boy who was outstanding. She'd not a single solitary one to invite.

It was easy enough for her mother to say that she could ask a boy from one of her classes, but then it would get around school that Cheryl Kramer was hard up for dates. When a girl had to come out cold and invite a boy who had scarcely looked at her twice, there was apt to be gossip about it. Besides, she'd have to stand him after they got to the dance, and it might mean she'd have to suffer through a whole evening of boredom and strained conversation.

Peter Guinness might come if she asked him, but then again he might not. Besides, she didn't even know whether he danced; probably he scorned dancing as he did so many other of the more common amusements. He'd be more fun than most, but it would be like him to come in tennis shoes and a sweat shirt, although he might have half a dozen suits in his closet. No, Peter was out of the question. She could not be seen at the dance with someone who resembled a "beach bum" when her mother had been trying all season to teach the Girls' Club the correct forms of social behavior. Peter, with his unconventional ways, would set a very poor example.

She was mulling over the problem as she left school on Friday afternoon, knowing that she had only a few more days in which to solve it, when Peter surprised her. He'd driven all the way from The Palisades in time to pick her up at the high school. The setting was as perfect as any Cheryl could have desired: gorgeous new foreign sports car, a boy behind the wheel shouting to her to hurry up and help him celebrate, and Ethel Barnes watching.

Sports cars of this expensive make were not common at Hunterford High. As Cheryl climbed in beside him, she was deliciously aware that she was creating a major sensation. For Ethel's benefit, she cuddled close to Peter and ran a hand through his hair. They roared off in a cloud of blue smoke from the exhaust pipes, and Cheryl hoped that Ethel had been standing close enough to be stifled. She smiled at the thought.

Once out of sight, she moved away from Peter, who seemed puzzled at this public show of affection, and listened to what he had to say. He had received the car yesterday as a birthday present; he had his full driver's license; and he was taking her out for dinner.

"But—but—" Cheryl was scarcely dressed for such an occasion.

"But nothing. We're driving straight down the shore to the yacht club. Here's a dime so you can call your mother." Peter swept grandly into a filling station with a pay telephone.

It was, as she told Judy and Alicia later, all sort of glorious and all completely mad. It had been like flying to drive in this sports car. And it had been crazy to go into the yacht club in nothing but their regular school clothes when everyone else in the dining room was dressed to the teeth.

"They're just people," Peter had said, leading the way to one of the head tables. "I choose to ignore them."

And then they had run out of gas on a long, deserted stretch of the coastline and had to walk simply miles through the dark. Cheryl's mother and father had been frantic and had sat up to wait for them.

"And then what do you suppose?" Cheryl paused in her account and left her listeners to guess.

Judy and Alicia were impatient and did a poor job of guessing. They urged her to finish.

"Well, Mother asked me whether Peter and I were serious about each other. Now isn't that a real laugh?"

"Well, aren't you? I was thinking the very same thing." Alicia could see nothing at all funny about it.

"Peter isn't that kind of a boy . . . at least not for me," Cheryl answered, not wishing to slight him. "He's fun to be with and all that, but he doesn't, well, exactly send me."

When her mother asked her to stop by at Bunting's on her way home from school and see what window decorations the store was prepared to offer them for the dance, she was reluctant to do it. She might run into Bill Meyers, and what was the use? She wished her mother would forget the whole affair. But that scarcely seemed likely. Mother had announced it at their latest session at the Club, and the girls were very excited.

Now, as she waited in the corridor outside the executive office of the store for someone to take her to the loft where the decorations were kept, she wanted to be almost anywhere else. Bill Meyers was coming toward her; he had been assigned to this task. He had never looked more appealing.

Her mother had said that she wanted to have a grand march and had asked Cheryl to look for something dramatic such as this cherry blossom arbor she'd spotted. The arbor could be marvelously romantic for the grand march and later, too, if you had the right partner, Cheryl thought, standing under it halfheartedly to test it for height.

It was then that Bill Meyers ventured a remark with a hesitance that was very unlike him. "I've got something sort of goofy to say, and it may make you laugh but—but you look like the spirit of springtime. Spring songs . . . birds . . . I don't know."

"Why, Bill, I didn't know that you cared," Cheryl said tritely, attempting to keep her voice from trembling and to sound gay and lighthearted.

"I didn't either—until this very minute. No, to be honest with you, it's been quite a while. I guess since that first day we met."

He came close and put his arms around her. Thank goodness the man in charge of store displays had gone about other business and left them alone.

"There's something so fresh and pretty about you, Cheryl. I can't quite explain it, but—but—" Again Bill hesitated. "I'll put up all the decorations for you if you'll let me take you to that dance."

"Will Ethel let you out for it?" Wickedly, Cheryl drew slightly away from him.

"I'm tired of having Ethel order me around. And I'm dead sick of all this phony, artificial sorority stuff she tries to pull on me. We broke up last week, you see. Now I'm walking out of it entirely. I—I want a girl with real heart and feelings."

"And so?" Cheryl lifted her face.

"How about giving it a try . . . just the two of us?"

"Let's," Cheryl murmured as Bill kissed her.

It was quite as wonderful as she had always dreamed it would be.

WHITMAN TEEN NOVELS

"Minnow" Vail

The Charmed Circle

Milestone Summer

When Sara Smiled

Practically Twins

Then Came November

When Debbie Dared

The Wishing Year